The
SECRET
OF THE
CIBOLO

The
SECRET OF THE CIBOLO

By Billie P. Matthews and A. Lee Chichester

EAKIN PRESS ★ Austin, Texas

FIRST EDITION

Copyright © 1988
by Billie Pipkin Matthews and A. Lee Chichester

Published in the United States of America
By Eakin Press, P.O. Box 23069, Austin, Texas 78735

ISBN 0-89015-638-7

Preface

The year is 1913 when an extraordinary Mexican arrives at El Rancho del Cibolo, owned by young Carlos Garcia's father. Many of the *tejano* vaqueros know that the man, who calls himself Pablo Gonzales, is actually the famous Gregorio Cortez, a legend among his people.

Twelve years before, Cortez was sent to prison for killing the sheriff who shot his brother, Romaldo. Even though pardoned, Cortez wants to remain anonymous due to the fact that some people — including the father of Carlos's best friend, Billy Baker — still believe that Cortez shot the sheriff in cold blood. But Carlos discovers Pablo's true identity and swears Billy to secrecy before telling him about Cortez and about the legendary collection of gold coins which he was supposed to have hidden during his ten-day, 600-mile flight from law officers back in 1901.

Pablo's good deeds and personal efforts to help the ranch cement an enduring friendship between himself and young Carlos and his family. That's why Carlos is distressed when Pablo says he must move on.

Although this story is fiction, Gregorio Cortez was a real figure in Mexican history.

[1]

"Come on, Billy. Let's see if there's enough water to fish," Carlos Garcia said.

The two boys tied their horses to a shade tree, grabbed the fishing poles, and clambered down the steep bank to the Cibolo River. Snuffling in the parched undergrowth, Pepe crashed down the bank after them and lapped from the trickle of water. No longer was the Cibolo a good-sized stream flowing through the Garcia spread, just east of San Antonio, Texas. The countryside was gripped by a terrible drought, and many of the local ranchers were already in financial trouble.

"Where will the fish go when there's no water?" asked Carlos's best friend, Billy Baker. Carlos shook his head.

Spying a backwash eddy downstream, Carlos led the way, hopping over a few rocks. The boys settled themselves beside the pool, lowered their baited hooks, and sat back to wait for a hungry fish.

As he stared at the cork float, Carlos thought about how worried his father looked these days. "Papa ought to

1

get away and come down here with us to fish," said Carlos. "He carries his cares on his shoulders like a packhorse."

Billy nodded. "If it isn't one thing it's another, these days."

Carlos knew that Billy was being kind enough to avoid details. He pushed from his mind the memory of the blackleg disease that ran like wildfire through their 300-head herd of mixed breed cattle last year. He and Billy never spoke of the huge piles of burning corpses or the smell. All that remained was a core group of expectant cows and cows with calves. They were lucky to be out on the farthest reaches of the Garcias' 900-acre spread and were spared the agony of the disease.

"Well, Carlos. Like my mama says, 'Necessity is a great teacher.' Today, your father has two new bulls, which are good foundation stock. The head count is up to 250, including newborns. That's not bad!"

Papa and the ranch foreman had just begun to relax after the blackleg when it became obvious that a drought was threatening the region. Now all the adults were worried again, and work for everyone had doubled. Even over at the Baker ranch, bordering Carlos's place on the south, they were saying that this was the worst drought anyone had seen for eighty years.

"Drat this drought!" complained Billy. "I hate having only one day a week that we can get together and have some fun."

Carlos nodded. Glancing upstream, he could almost see the water evaporating. "The river seems lower today than when we were here last," he said. Today was the eighty-third straight day without a hope of rain.

Pepe, who had flopped onto a shady rock to recover from the dusty, hot run to the Cibolo, jerked his head upright and pricked his ears. Carlos didn't hear anything, but he trusted his dog to be on to something. Nudging Billy with his elbow, he placed a finger to his lips. Waiting motionless, they expected a thirsty armadillo or raccoon to emerge from the mesquite. Finally, they heard a rustling in the woods. Above, on top of the bank, the horses neighed, and the boys were surprised to hear an answering whinny.

Pepe leapt up and began barking furiously. He snarled and growled, keeping himself protectively between Carlos and the high bank at his back. Carlos and Billy stood and shielded their eyes, trying to discover the cause of the commotion. A figure appeared, looking down at them from the high bank a little downstream. Wearing a *sombrero,* he stood next to a huge, old hollow pecan that had been dead for years. He disappeared into the undergrowth, then reappeared directly above them, leading his horse down the rocky trail to the riverbed.

"Hush, Pepe. Just a stranger passing through. Now be quiet, mind your manners —"

Carlos's scoldings were cut short when Billy jumped back and shouted, "Carlos, look! Your cork!" Carlos scrambled to grab the pole before it slipped into the pool.

Struggling with the angry fish, Carlos tried to tune out the racket of all that was going on around him. Pepe was still barking while Billy danced about with excitement. Then the stranger began issuing instructions of his own: "Careful now, *jovencito!* Ease him on in . . . easy now." Carlos was an expert fisherman. He needed no help to land the enormous catfish.

"Wow, this must be the granddaddy of them all! He's huge!" exclaimed Billy.

"He must be twelve pounds!" said Carlos.

The stranger threw back his head and cut loose with a loud laugh.

"You have caught an excellent meal for us, *jovencito,*" he said. "That is, if you will share it with one so humble as myself." He bowed, removing his *sombrero* with a sweep of his leathery hand.

The boys considered the man before them: the thick, black mustache on a deeply tanned face, the amused amber eyes, the close-cropped but curly, sweaty hair. He was tall and slender with slightly stooped shoulders. He dressed nicely, in the usual *tejano* way, with a *serape* across his shoulder, but he had the dust-encrusted look of a traveler who had covered many miles.

Finally, Carlos spoke. "This is part of *El Rancho del Cibolo,* owned by my parents. My name is Carlos Garcia. Are you lost or just passing through?"

The stranger's eyes danced with gaiety. "Oh, my friend! What luck! This is the exact ranch I was searching for. I've come to stay with my friend, Juan Garcia — your own father!"

"Have we met before, *señor?*" Carlos asked.

A seriousness passed through the stranger's eyes, and he hesitated before replying. "Perhaps we have. My name is Pablo. Pablo Gonzales," he said softly. He lowered his intense gaze and looked at the fish, still on Carlos's line. "But we should clean that fish, my friend. I'd be pleased to build a small fire and supply the fry pan if you will share your hard-won catch with me."

The boys looked at each other. Satisfied that this stranger meant them no harm, they set about looking for firewood.

After they had eaten, Pablo doused his face and hair with water from the fishing pool. Carlos smothered the fire with sand and pebbles. They had all been very hungry and had easily polished off the meal. Pepe waited expectantly for scraps, but he had to satisfy himself with the fleshless, hard-boned, and sharp-whiskered head of the catfish.

The evening sun was dropping below the far edge of the riverbank when Carlos said, "We must hurry. My parents will worry if it gets too dark, and we've a long way to go to get to my house."

As they neared the hub of activity on the ranch, Carlos indicated the small frame dwellings and explained, "These are where our traveling *vaqueros* live."

"And who lives in that adobe, my friend?"

"No one right now. That's the original house that my

ancestors built, back before Texas was a republic. My family was among the first real settlers to come to this territory. Up until the 1730s, only soldiers and missionaries lived here. But it was my," Carlos paused to count on his fingers, "great-great-great-great-grandfather who was the first *hidalgo* to own this land."

"And up there is where the Garcia ancestors are buried," offered Billy. He pointed toward a high, overgrown mound next to a modest chapel.

Pablo nodded and gently spurred his mount to a trot. "We must hurry. The darkness approaches."

They reined up at the edge of a clearing in front of a frame house. As they dismounted, the large Garcia family, as well as several visiting *tejanos,* came out and stood quietly in the yard area. Carlos watched them assemble. The men at the front removed their *sombreros* and kept their eyes on the ground. The women hushed the children and hovered in the back, little ones clinging to their skirts.

Only Juan Garcia came forward and, with a broad smile, clapped Pablo in a huge *abrazo.* "You are just in time for dinner, my friend."

At once, Carlos knew that this was no ordinary man. He was an honored guest at his father's home! Feeling very proud, he said, "Papa. Billy, Pablo, and I have already eaten —"

"And I've got to go now, or Pa will have my hide!" interrupted Billy.

"Thank you, Billy, for escorting — Pablo — to my home. He is a very special friend to us."

Carlos watched Billy mount and jog off toward his family's ranch.

"Now, my son, you must go explain to your mother why you ate dinner already when you knew that she was fixing your favorite — *cabrito.* Pablo and I have some catching up to do." Juan ushered Carlos inside as the crowd of visitors surrounded Pablo, all talking at once.

"I'm sorry, Mother. I forgot all about the dinner. I

5

caught this huge catfish, and with Pablo's arrival and everything — I just wasn't thinking."

"You are an ungrateful son, Carlitos," she teased. "I've been working all day to roast the meat and here you've already eaten. Next time you ask for *cabrito* I'll consider long and hard before I consent to cook it for you." She continued clucking and scolding him.

Carlos listened with only half an ear as he helped carry plates of food to the table. His mind was on the curious stranger they had met at the riverside. There was something grand about him — something larger-than-life. But Carlos couldn't think of why he might be so important — so honored.

Several times during the loud, chattering chaos of dinner, Carlos caught himself staring rudely at the stranger. All of the guests treated him like nobility, serving him first and jumping at his every whim. But they enthusiastically talked to him about everyday life on the ranch — from the problems of the drought to the engagements of the young people. Carlos was mystified.

The women had retired and most of the guests had gone home by the time Carlos was sent off to bed. The only ones still gathered around the large dining table were his father, Pablo, and the ranch foreman, Alonzo.

Usually, a steady warm breeze blew through Carlos's bedroom because the windows were thrown wide during the summer. But tonight, all was still. Even the night noises were muffled, as if everything was being still and silent enough to reserve every drop of water. Carlos opened up his door a little to catch any cross breeze that might come his way.

The discussion coming from the dining room, which Carlos couldn't help but overhear, was about politics. Mostly it had to do with Mexico and the border troubles farther south. But Carlos couldn't understand some of their murmurings.

". . . feelings are still running high in this territory." His father was talking now. "We must not let anyone know of your true identity."

At this, Carlos strained to hear more. Now he knew the stranger was more than what he seemed!

"Our neighbors, the Bakers, are . . . *Señor* Baker was among the posse which you led on a merry chase . . . does not speak of it, but I believe he is a man who carries a grudge."

". . . twelve years ago . . ." Carlos could not make out the soft tones, but he recognized Pablo's voice. And then Alonzo spoke for the first time. His voice was high-pitched and easily understood.

"You were wise to disguise your real name, Gregorio — I mean Pablo." Carlos heard them chuckle. "It is best that we keep your name quiet, even among our people. Some of them often talk more than they listen."

Carlos searched his mind for ways to fit the pieces of the story together. Twelve years . . . Gregorio . . . posse . . . escape. Pablo was speaking again, and Carlos could hear none of it. Finally, the conversation meandered off to voting — for what or whom, Carlos couldn't catch. His eyelids became heavy, and he drifted off to sleep, dreaming of mystery and adventure.

It was still velvety dark when Carlos felt Papa's forceful hand shaking him awake. Breakfast was finished before the sun rose, and the working day began. Just at sunrise, Papa met on the front porch with Alonzo and a few other key *vaqueros*, outlining their tasks for the day. But there was a new face in the gathering.

"*Buenos días,* everyone," began Papa. "This is my good friend, Pablo Gonzales. He is here from San Antonio and will be working with us for a short while."

Those who had not been present at the previous night's meal greeted Pablo courteously. Papa spoke to Pablo when he continued. "Carlos has a huge chore to attend this morning, and he carries lunch to the hands every day. You will be paired with him for now since Alonzo and I have to cross the river this morning." He turned toward Carlos and resumed, "I want you and Pablo to clear out the cemetery of the dead weeds and

8

brambles. It's an insult to our ancestors to have all those dried grasses on the graves — you can't even see the tombstones."

"*Sí, señor.*" Carlos knew the job would take hours. I'll never be done in time to go fishing or lizard-hunting with Billy, he thought, scuffing his boot in the dust.

But when he looked up at Pablo, his disappointment evaporated. Carlos smiled when he received a reassuring wink. At least I won't be doing it alone, he thought. It'll go faster with two, and maybe I can figure out who he really is.

Carlos showed Pablo around the main working area of the ranch, with faithful Pepe following at their heels. As they neared the yellowed vegetable garden, Carlos and Pepe saw one of the stray cats crouching in the patch, intent on capturing an insect. Pepe took off like a streak to give chase, but ended up dancing and barking at the base of the tree where the cat escaped.

Carlos and Pablo laughed at his frustration and rode on, past the withering orchard and the dried-up creek bed. Heading toward the chapel, Pablo hesitated beside the old adobe. "*Jovencito,* would it be arrogant of me to ask if I could live in your great-great-great-great-grandfather's house? It would be good to have my own place."

"Oh, no! Papa would love it if you could get some use out of it. The place hasn't been used for years, so it is probably a mess. The last time we checked the well was when cattle were pastured up here, so I don't know if the drought has dried it up or not."

"Why don't we find out?"

They stopped by the back of the house and lowered the metal bucket on a rope into the well.

"It is low, but with care, water can still be drawn," announced Pablo with a smile. He offered the bit of water he had raised to Pepe. "I will make sure my selection of a home is approved by your father before I move in."

He's so polite, marveled Carlos as they mounted and

moved off toward the chapel on the rise. Perhaps he is from the nobility of Mexico!

The cemetery was worse than Carlos had imagined. Dead dewberry brambles matted the brown grasses in the corners. A scrubby mesquite tree offered limited shade to the tall, strawlike covering over the graves. The ancient stone wall surrounding them was tumbling down in several places.

They dismounted and tied the horses on the shady side of the chapel. "It looks hopeless, Pablo," complained Carlos. He walked over to the rusty iron gate and pushed. The scrub beneath prevented it from swinging on its hinges. He pulled instead, and the gate grudgingly opened for him.

"My great-great-great-great-grandfather said he wanted to be buried facing the chapel. That tall stone is his marker," said Carlos, indicating a fingerlike monument reaching out of the overgrowth toward the sky. "But you can't even see the chapel from there with all this brush in the way."

Carlos high-stepped over toward the gravestone, but froze, gasping and wide-eyed. He was staring straight into the reptilian eyes of a surprised copperhead. Behind him, Pepe sensed his panic and barked ferociously, almost drawing the snake's attention away from Carlos.

"Don't move, my friend," said Pablo quietly, on his left. A shattering pistol report made Carlos duck his head just as the copperhead was going to strike. It never hit its mark, though, as its head was blown back and destroyed. Carlos couldn't move a muscle; his eyes were locked on the writhing of the headless serpent.

At last the breath he had held deep in his lungs during the ordeal escaped. He wiped his brow with the back of his hand and glanced at Pablo, who was replacing the pistol beneath his *serape* in a holster.

"That was close, *jovencito,*" said Pablo, placing an arm around Carlos's shoulders. "Come sit for a while."

10

He led the unsteady boy over to a stone bench near the wall.

"Where'd you learn to shoot like that, Pablo?" Carlos whispered, unsure of his voice.

"Oh, in my family, we learn as young boys how to shoot and ride. It is part of the Cortez culture, because for so long our neighbor, Mexico, has been in chaos. Down on the border we live so close to fighting that we must always be prepared to defend ourselves."

"Can you teach me? Can you show me how to shoot?"

Pablo laughed at Carlos's enthusiasm. "Certainly, my friend. I will teach you to handle a pistol sometime. But today, we must finish the job here. Let me take one of the boards I saw lying near the chapel and scare off any remaining snakes. You wait here and try to recover."

Carlos felt better. Slowly, it dawned on him that Pablo had slipped and told him his real last name. Gregorio Cortez! He knew the stranger's story immediately, and was astonished and amazed to be working so closely with such a legend. He took a deep breath and went to the nearby shed and grabbed a scythe and a hoe. Gregorio Cortez in the flesh! Carlos had always heard about this living hero, but never dreamed he'd meet him face-to-face.

Suddenly, Carlos could hardly remember why they had come to the cemetery in the first place. But the antics of his working partner reminded him. Pablo was beating his board on the grasses in the cemetery, repeatedly shouting *"Vayáte!"* He looked so funny, waving that huge board and yelling, that Carlos started laughing uncontrollably. Pablo heard him and began scolding him, waving his arms around and smiling while still flailing the board around. Carlos laughed all the harder, even though he knew it was impolite to laugh at one so revered as Gregorio Cortez. Finally, he had to sit down in the weeds, holding his stomach as tears streamed down his cheeks.

When the giggles subsided, he rose and began hack-

11

ing at the grass near the wall. Pablo took the hoe and up-
rooted brambles in the corner. Soon, Pablo was humming
a tune that Carlos remembered hearing just recently. He
recognized it as a ballad that one of the *vaqueros* had
sung quietly under the moon. It had seemed so solemn
that Carlos remembered holding his breath, trying to
hear the words, but he was unable to distinguish them.

It was a nice tune that went with the rythmic hack-
ing and weeding they were doing. Carlos forgot the incident with the snake, thinking only of how — and if — he
should tell Billy of his new discovery.

The work went much quicker than Carlos had believed it would. With his thoughts cascading like a river
along a turbulent path, he didn't hear the sound of approaching hoofbeats. He looked up, and there was Billy.

"Hey, Carlos! Are you almost finished? I'd like to try
to get that catfish's brother today, if we can."

"But after this, I must return to the house and
gather the lunches to take to the *vaqueros* . . ." Carlos
could think of no way to escape, and he still wasn't sure
whether he should tell Billy the big news.

"Don't worry, my friend," offered Pablo. "I'll take the
lunches today. It will be a good way for me to meet more
of the workers. You go to your fishing hole with your
friend. Some things between boys cannot wait for the set-
ting of the sun."

"Oh, thank you, Pablo. I'll return the favor, I promise."

He mounted his horse and galloped ahead of Billy,
weighing the seriousness of his decision to tell his friend
about Gregorio.

[3]

Carlos and Billy rode swiftly down to the banks of the river. Carlos was silent as thoughts churned through his mind. The boys scrambled down the steep bank and Carlos walked along the dried riverbed, looking for what, he did not know.

At last, he stopped and squatted down on his haunches atop a large boulder that overlooked a wide beach. High on the bank was the hull of the majestic pecan tree — dead for years and hollowed out from above eye level to the jagged top where the branches used to be. It was a special tree that Carlos and Billy had come to know while playing and hunting along the Cibolo.

"What's wrong, Carlos?" asked Billy breathlessly.

Carlos remained silent, surveying the banks, the tree, and the trickle of water that used to be a swift river.

"So many things change, *amigo,*" he finally said. "Trees die and grow hollow. Rivers shrink and cease their singing. But friendship — that must never change! Do you agree?"

13

"Of course I do. We're *hermanos de la sangre;* we mixed our blood a long time ago, remember?"

Carlos simply nodded, still not looking at Billy. Then they both scrambled down the far side of the boulder and landed on the sand.

Carlos began collecting medium-sized rocks from along the banks of the river. He brought each one to the center of the flat area and carefully arranged them, just touching. First they formed an arc, then a semicircle.

"What are you doing, Carlos? The fish are waiting."

But Carlos kept collecting. He knew that the stage had to be set. Billy must understand how important his silence would be. He must know that this was not a mere fishing expedition.

At last, still intent on his job, Carlos said, "There is a bond between us that will never be broken. We have shared and mingled our blood, this is true. But what I am going to tell you now goes beyond blood. You will have to ignore your own heritage in this one instance, and fully adopt mine. In becoming *un hidalgo* in this, it will be like protecting one of your own. You will do more than protect your blood brother; you will protect your people."

Carlos completed the circle of rocks. He then took out his hunting knife and dove into the underbrush along the bank. Fighting canes and branches in the still, hot undergrowth, he finally found what he was searching for. He cut a long strand of vine and stripped it of leaves and bark as he emerged, sweat glistening on his forehead.

"Come into the circle, *amigo.*"

Carlos carefully removed several stones to make an opening in the circle. Billy stepped inside and Carlos followed, stooping to close up the opening again. He twined the vine around Billy's left wrist and turned his palm up. Then he twined the rest of the vine around his own right wrist and tightened it so that their pulse-points touched and their hands were crossed. They faced the east, the west, the north, then the south.

"Brothers yesterday, brothers today, brothers tomorrow. Brothers in the east, brothers in the west, brothers in the north, and brothers in the south." Again, they turned each direction of the compass as Carlos said the lilting words.

"This circle of trust can never be broken."

"Never be broken," replied Billy.

"Brothers forever."

"Para siempre."

At last, Carlos slipped his knife between their hands and in one motion sliced the vine. It untwined from their hands, and he bent down to remove the rocks for the opening again. When they were outside, Carlos carefully closed up the circle and tossed his part of the vine inside. Billy did the same.

"What I am going to tell you is a story that only my people know from beginning to end — yet it is not ended even now. The rumors that your people hear and tell are not the facts. You will have to decide for yourself which tale you will accept as your own. For me, the tale that follows is what I know to be true.

"Two years before you or I were born, twelve years ago, a very peaceful, hard-working, range-riding man lived in Karnes County, just south of here. His name was Gregorio Cortez. He lived with his wife and four children, as well as his older brother Romaldo and his wife.

"One day, Sheriff Morris came to call on them, asking about a horse that either Gregorio or Romaldo had traded earlier that day. The sad part of the story is about a man named Boone Choate, who went along with Sheriff Morris to translate for him. He is the sad part because he didn't know Spanish very well. When he asked Gregorio if he'd traded a *caballo* that day, Gregorio honestly answered 'no' because he'd traded a *yegua* instead."

"Any *vaquero* would know the difference between a male and a female horse," observed Billy.

"Boone Choate didn't know the difference in the words. Another sad event was when Sheriff Morris decided that he had to arrest Gregorio and take him into

15

town for questioning. Gregorio was within his rights when he said, 'You cannot arrest me for nothing.' But Boone Choate translated this to the sheriff as, 'No man can arrest me.'

"Sheriff Morris stood up to the challenge and pulled his gun. To protect his brother, the unarmed Romaldo took a dive at the sheriff but was shot for his efforts. With his brother wounded on the ground, Gregorio pulled his own gun and shot the sheriff. Boone Choate quickly rode away to tell the town that Gregorio Cortez had shot Sheriff Morris in cold blood."

"Yeah, I remember now," interrupted Billy. "Pa said that this Cortez was a 'sheriff-slayer.' "

Carlos was silent for a while, shaking his head slightly. Then he continued.

"By walking and riding ten miles into town, Gregorio managed to get the badly wounded Romaldo to a doctor. The rest of his family was held in jail when the posse caught up with them, but Gregorio escaped by making a long and perilous two-day journey afoot to a friend's house some eighty miles north. But along the way, he was housed and fed by friends and strangers alike."

"Whatever happened to Romaldo?"

"He died a little later — not right away, and not of his wounds, they say." Carlos paused for a moment, then continued. "There, at the Schnabel ranch, where his friend lived, and under the confusion of darkness, Gregorio was ambushed. Another sheriff was killed, but few are sure that it was Gregorio who shot him. Again he fled, this time taking a southwestern route, and this time on horseback.

"He passed eight more days in this way: sleeping little, eating on the run, hiding in the chaparral. In fact, he even crossed the Cibolo during that time. Some say that it was right here in this area where he crossed!"

"Do you think so?"

Carlos shrugged.

"His little sorrel mare was big-hearted and willing.

16

In the end, she carried him over 500 miles. Along the way, our people heard of his distress and gave him hospitality, food, shelter. If it wasn't for the kindness of these people, he could not have made it as far as he did."

"You mean he didn't make it across the border?"

"A traitor to his cause and to our people turned him in — for a fee which he was never able to spend, it had so much blood on it." Carlos spit in the sand for emphasis. "By some miracle, Gregorio was not lynched when he was caught. He had a series of trials and in the end was sent to Huntsville prison for nine years, but only after first spending three years on the trials and in jail cells."

"Twelve whole years — wow. What ever became of him?"

Carlos searched Billy's face with piercing eyes. "Before I tell you that, let me put the tail on this story." He looked around them suspiciously and dropped his voice. "It is said that during his flight, Gregorio was given coins — just one or two at a time — by the people who wanted to help him escape. He was the first *tejano* to stand up for the rights of his family on his own property, and our people loved him instantly. He collected a whole *morral* of these gold coins, they say, but he carried no money when he went into Huntsville. It is said that he hid it — buried it or left it with a trusted friend — along the path of his flight."

"But what happened? I can tell by your face that the best is yet to come!"

Carlos smiled. "You know me like a brother, *amigo*. All right. The best part is this. He's actually here — Gregorio Cortez is staying at El Rancho del Cibolo."

"Pablo?"

"*Sí!*"

"Wow!"

"He has been given a pardon after all this time in prison." Carlos grinned, then he grew serious again. "As my brother, you will tell no one of his true name. Not my father nor yours nor Pablo himself must know that you know. There would be but one conclusion they could draw. They'd know that I had told you, and I will not be thought a traitor!" Carlos spit again in disgust.

"The secret is safe with me. I know you believe in me or you would never have told me in the first place. I will not betray you or your people."

"Our people."

"Yes, our people."

Carlos glanced to the circle of stones and felt the weight of secrecy on his shoulders for a minute. But now he felt much better, having shared the secret. Then he thought with excitement, I know a legend!

His pulse quickened and he glanced at Billy, who was obviously still awed by this revelation. "I don't feel much like fishing, do you?"

Billy just shook his head.

[4]

Carlos looked forward to the occasional days that he and Pablo worked together. The problem was, Pablo was such a good worker that everyone on the ranch wanted to work with him. Alonzo enlisted him to chop the stunted hay, Papa rode with him to the far pastures, and even Mama had him toting barrels of grain or buckets of water around the house.

At least Carlos always got to see and talk to Pablo when he took the lunches to the fields and barns. He was careful to keep his secret to himself, although he couldn't help stealing lingering looks at the man who was a living legend.

One day Carlos rushed out of the house and down to the Baker place. "Billy! Where's Billy?"

Mrs. Baker looked alarmed. "What is it, Carlos? Billy has gone with his father into town for supplies. Are you . . ."

But Carlos couldn't wait for her to finish. Racing into the field where Pablo and Papa were filling a trough with river water for the cattle, he noticed that Papa

19

looked at his watch, expecting lunch. But he couldn't worry about that now. His main concern was Pepe — he hadn't eaten his food from yesterday morning and no one had seen him for over twenty-four hours.

"Papa! Pablo! Pepe still isn't back. I'm awfully worried! His food is just sitting on the back porch, drawing flies. I know you told me to wait until sundown, Papa, but I just can't stop worrying about him. What if he's in trouble or . . . or worse." Carlos tried to fight the tears welling up in his eyes, but he lost the battle. He turned his head so his father couldn't see his face. Motioning back toward the house, he said, "I've already looked and looked . . ."

"Well, *jovencito*. Let's just go and look again, *sí?*"

Papa nodded to Pablo. "I can handle this from here, *amigo*," he said.

Swinging up on his horse, Pablo grabbed Carlos's arm and helped him up behind the saddle. They galloped off toward the house.

The first place they looked was under the house. No Pepe. They tried the barn, the smokehouse, and the corncrib. No sign of him.

"You've tried calling him, Carlitos?"

"Yes. Lots of times. *Pepe! Here Pepe!*"

"Let us tack up your horse and ride down to check the orchard. Maybe he has holed up in there, where there is more shade."

They looked around the orchard and in the cemetery. They checked the *vaqueros'* yards, beside the old windmill, and in every building around the central area.

"The only place left is down by the river, or somewhere along the way, my friend. Let's take a ride."

They had barely gotten out of the near pasture when Carlos reined up and said, "Shhh!"

Even the horses pricked their ears to listen. Then they heard it. A weak whine made Carlos cock his head, trying to figure out where it was coming from. He and Pablo glanced around, hoping to hear it again.

20

"I think it was coming from that clump of bushes," suggested Carlos. "Pepe? Pepe!"

Then they heard it again, louder. Carlos spurred his horse to the overgrowth in the corner of the pasture. Throwing himself onto the ground in such haste that he nearly fell down, Carlos raced to the bushes and skidded to a stop. He dropped to his knees to find a pitiful Pepe stretched out full length in the shade.

"Oh, Pepe! What happened?"

The dog's forepaw was encrusted with blood. Flies swarmed around the wound. Pepe was too weak to twitch them away.

"There, there, *perrito*," cooed Pablo. He waved the flies away from the paw and gently cradled it, examining the damage. Pepe didn't even lift his head. "Get him some water from my saddle, *jovencito*. See if he will take any. I'm afraid he's very sick."

Carlos raced to the gut bag that Pablo always carried full of water. He returned, spilling it into his hand and holding it under Pepe's nose. His glazed eyes opened a crack, but he didn't drink.

"Will he be all right?" Carlos asked. "He won't take any water. What could have happened to him?"

"It looks like a trap wound. Has your papa had trouble with small animals around the ranch?"

"Near the corncrib we've been getting visits from a raccoon or something. I think Papa told me that he'd put out a trap. Could that be it?"

"It's possible, *amigo*. Let's get Pepe back to the house where you can make him more comfortable."

"Will he be all right, Pablo?" whispered Carlos.

"Nature has a way of taking care of her own. And this is a fine, strong dog. Let us see how nature works her miracles. Only time will tell."

Carlos tried to coax Pepe out from under the bushes, but the dog was too weak to move more than one limb at a time. Finally, Pablo gently scooted him into the sun and carefully picked him up in his arms.

Leading Pablo's horse the short way back to the house, Carlos jogged home. He had managed to fix up a makeshift bed for Pepe by the time Pablo reached the porch with his limp cargo. Although he put food and water near where the dog could reach them, Carlos still couldn't get him to drink.

Mama fixed an herbal mixture to clean the wound, and Carlos worked carefully on Pepe's paw to remove the blood and dirt. Pepe twitched several times and looked at him but flopped back in exhaustion.

"I think he knows I'm trying to help him," he said to Pablo.

"I'm sure he does, *jovencito*. You stay and do your best now. I will take over the lunches today. It's way past noon, and I think maybe some *vaqueros* will be very hungry by now."

"Oh, thank you, Pablo. I forgot all about that."

He continued working on the dog — rinsing his cloth in the herbs, pressing it onto the wound, and rinsing it again.

When he thought he'd done all he could for the wound, he concentrated on getting Pepe to drink. The boy dipped his finger into the water and dropped it onto Pepe's dry, black nose. Finally, he lapped tiredly from Carlos's cupped palm.

At last, Billy returned from town and began sharing the vigil with Carlos. They sat together with Pepe through the night. Mama brought them food and water to help pass the time and keep up their strength.

The days passed, and the boys knew that sitting beside their old friend could do no more good. Carlos was still responsible for his chores, even though most of the time he was distracted with worry. Billy worked twice as hard as before, finishing his own duties first, then dealing with Carlos's chores. Even Papa and Mama, and sometimes Pablo, finished Carlos's work when he couldn't keep his mind on it.

The boy's absent-mindedness grew daily as it became apparent that Pepe was getting worse. On the sixth day, Papa took Carlos aside after dinner.

"Son, it's hard to see your old friend suffer, I know. None of us want to see him in pain. That's like torture. You know what we always do with a horse or a steer that's broken his leg? Do you know why we choose to destroy the animal?"

"Why?" Carlos croaked, staring blindly at his feet.

"Because the animal will suffer while it tries to mend, but it will never get better. Do you understand?"

Carlos nodded.

"We may be forced to do the same to old Pepe, because it's much better for him if we put him out of his torture, instead of allowing his suffering to continue."

"No, Papa, please! Just one more day. Please!" Carlos felt the panic welling up inside him. His mouth tasted sour with his fear for Pepe. The tears came again, but Carlos was past caring about them. "Can't we do something?"

"Son, I'm afraid that a bad infection has set in. If it has gone too far we cannot cure it."

"But in a day, he might be better. Please?" Carlos was whispering now.

He waited for what seemed like an eternity before his father said, "All right. But if he's not better by tomorrow night, we'll have to put him down."

Completely dejected, Carlos sat on the porch next to Billy. He knew that his friend had heard the awful truth.

"Don't give up, *hermano*. There is still hope," said Billy.

The dog slipped in and out of fitful sleep, moaning sometimes. Carlos's hand brushed away the tears until he could hold back the sobs no longer. He clutched at the quilts on which his old friend lay dying.

Silent tears streamed down Billy's face.

The morning found them curled up beside Pepe. They were awakened by Pablo's footsteps on the porch.

"My little friends," he whispered. "Let us give old Mother Nature a hand."

24

"What do you mean? Are you going to shoot Pepe?" asked Carlos.

"No, but *Señor* Garcia is right. We might have to if my little remedy does not help. He told me last night that the paw is infected."

"It is bad, Pablo."

"I do not believe there is anything worse than an infection. Once, a friend of mine was badly wounded from an accident on the trail. A local *curandera* knew an ancient Aztec healing potion made from a deadly plant. She saved his leg from being cut off."

Carlos's eyes widened. "Do you know the potion? Where can we get it? Will it work on Pepe?"

"Not so many questions, my friend." He smiled and hesitated. "It is a painful remedy, but strong. Since I learned of this miracle potion, I carry the dried powder in my saddlebags everywhere I go. Until now, I believed that I carried it simply as a good luck charm. But maybe Pepe can have some good luck from it."

Pablo slowly measured out the powder and carefully, drop by drop, added water. When it was a thick, gooey, mudlike mess, he scooped it out with a flat-sided stick and smeared it on Pepe's swollen paw. The dog whimpered and tried to raise his head enough to bite at his paw, but he was far too weak.

"If his strength returns, you must be certain that he never touches his mouth to this mixture. If he eats any, we certainly won't have to shoot him. He will die instantly."

Carlos's mouth dropped open. He wondered how something so deadly could do any good at all. But he knew they had to try anything that gave Pepe even a shred of hope.

By nightfall, Pepe's sleep was more comfortable. He drank quite a lot of water and even tried to eat a little.

"See, Papa?" exclaimed Carlos. "He's a little better, don't you think? Pablo may be able to save him. Can we give him another day? Please?"

Carlos knew his father had to admit that Pepe was

better. He leapt for joy when his father said, "We'll see how tomorrow goes, Carlos."

By the end of the week, with Pablo coming twice daily to administer the poultice, Pepe was less feverish and more lively. He even thumped his tail against the wooden porch in greeting when he saw Carlos. But Pepe grew to dislike the appearance of Pablo on the porch each time he came.

The dog was sitting up regularly, and he protested greatly when the medicine was placed on his paw. Carlos had a tough job of it, trying to keep Pepe's head away from his foot.

"Well, *jovencitos*," said Pablo one evening. "Our faithful follower has made a grand recovery. I don't think the potion will do any more good now. And anyway, I have almost run out. I'd like to keep a small bit to have as a charm, even though I am not a superstitious man." He tousled Carlos's hair and grinned, his amber eyes dancing. Billy beamed happily and clapped Carlos on the back.

"Thank you, Pablo. You saved Pepe," said Carlos. They glanced over toward the dog, who was cowering in the corner, staring cautiously at Pablo. Carlos laughed and said, "Now you'll have to make friends with Pepe again, Pablo!"

"That stuff must be really mean!" exclaimed Billy. "Here, give him this bit of beef fat that I saved from dinner."

Pablo talked in low, even tones to the dog. Pepe sat quietly, holding his paw up, expecting the worst. His tail thumped when Pablo gave him the treat and gently scratched his chest.

They knew it was just a matter of time now. Pretty soon Pepe would be chasing cats up trees and trotting after the boys on their jaunts to the river, scaring armadillos along the way. Pablo grinned over his shoulder at them and winked.

[5]

The drought lingered on, while Carlos's routine returned to normal. Pepe followed along again as Carlos
delivered lunches to the *vaqueros*. Everyone worked very
hard, trying to keep the animals watered and fed in the
harsh conditions. Lunchtime was a special, relaxing
break to all who labored under the broiling sun.

"Come, Carlitos!" called his mother. "There's one
very important lunch left for you to deliver, and you must
enjoy your own as well. Your papa is working alone in
the far pasture with the calves. Go now and spend a moment with him breaking bread together."

The boy was delighted to spend some quiet time
under a shade tree in a short *siesta* with Papa. He galloped out in the direction of the calves' run, leaving the
still weak Pepe resting on the porch.

Carlos pulled up short when he saw a horse, standing alone with his saddle and bridle still on, nibbling at
some mesquite.

"Whoa there, Octavio," he said as he recognized his
father's mount. "Where's Papa, old boy?" He expected to

see his father relaxing in the shade farther on. But he saw no signs of life.

"Papa?" he called. Then, reaching for the horse's reins, he realized that they were not tied up at all.

"*Papa?*" he shouted, becoming alarmed.

He noticed that the pasture gate was swinging freely, wide open. His father was never so careless. Knowing something was very wrong, Carlos searched the pasture, calling out now and then. But the silence told him that his father was nowhere near.

Fear gripped him as he spurred his horse back to the ranch house and called, "Pablo! Alonzo! Mama! I can't find Papa! *Ayuda, pronto, pronto!*"

A search party was quickly assembled, and Alonzo outlined everyone's duties. "Carlos, you go back to where you found Octavio and search thoroughly in that area. If you find nothing, bring the horse back, untack him, and give him some water. Pablo, you take Rafael and Karl to the calf run and look there. I'll take Michael and Juan with me to the next pasture to see what we can find. Everyone report back here in one hour."

In a cloud of dust, the searchers were off. They began combing the grounds and calling out into the silence.

Carlos rushed to Octavio again and crashed through the tangle of mesquite, hardly blinking when he ran smack into a prickly pear. There was no sign of his father. Carlos began to be afraid that maybe a rattlesnake had bitten Papa and that he was unconscious. He looked in the brush and along the fence. Finally, he was forced to admit defeat and return to the house. Octavio limped along behind him, and Carlos, shaking his head silently in response to his mother's anxious face, headed for the barn.

After tending to the horses' needs, he sat on the porch. There was still a while to go before the others were scheduled to be back. His mother sat with him, wringing her hands in a dish towel and mumbling distractedly.

"Don't worry, Mama. Papa will be fine, you'll see."

"Maybe I should get dinner started . . ."

"How about if I start the fire for you?"

"He's never late for meals . . ."

"Mama," Carlos went over to her and held her arm. "There's nothing you or I can do right now. Let's work on dinner."

But still she sat, knitting her hands in and out of the worn towel. Carlos decided to forget about dinner, and they passed the time searching the horizon for signs of the men.

At last, Pablo and his search party returned, dragging a makeshift litter behind one of the horses. Carlos and Mama raced into the yard to see Papa, pale and dusty, lying on the litter. Carlos could tell that he was in tremendous pain.

"We must get him gently inside," stated Pablo. "He has been without water for too long. Alonzo and Michael have gone to fetch a doctor."

"Alaba el cielo! He is alive!" exclaimed Carlos's mother, looking heavenward. She rushed ahead into the house to prepare the bedroom.

Carlos helped the men unhitch the litter and carry Papa into the house. Gently, they eased him onto the soft, still bed. He groaned from the pain.

"What is it?" asked Carlos. "A rattler bite?"

"No, *jovencito.* Your papa has taken a terrible fall from his horse. I'm certain that bones are broken, but I cannot tell if more serious damage has been done inside. The first thing he needs is a little water."

Carlos ran into the kitchen, where his mother was already preparing a pitcher and a washbowl. Carlos helped her carry the water back into the bedroom.

"All right. Everyone out," declared *Señora* Garcia. "I must wash him as best as I can and coax him to drink a little. You all wait on the porch for *el médico.*"

Mama bustled everyone out of the small room. She was no longer distracted or purposeless, now that she knew that Papa needed her. Carlos hovered near the entry until his mother shut the door in his face. Resigned to wait, he joined the others on the porch.

"Will he be all right, Pablo?"

"He is a strong man, *amigo*. Time will tell."

Shortly, Doc Starnes rode up in a whirlwind of dust and barged right into the house. They all looked helplessly at the doorway through which he disappeared. Carlos could stand it no longer. "Is there nothing we can do?" he asked, desperation cracking his voice.

"Yes, little friend," answered Pablo. "You can care for the doctor's horse while we wait."

Reluctantly, Carlos took the animal to the barn, where he loosened the girth and gave him some water. The sweat was foamy on his shoulders and flanks, so Carlos rubbed him with a burlap rag and walked him to cool down.

"Hey, Carlos! Where is everybody? The fields are empty except for a few thirsty cows . . ."

"Oh. Hi, Billy. Doc Starnes is in with Papa. He's taken a fall, and we don't know how bad he is yet."

"Geeze, Carlos! When did this happen?"

"We just found him about a half hour ago. I don't know how long he's been lying out there in the sun."

The boys went back to the porch to wait with the others. Finally, Doc Starnes came out, sleeves rolled up and sweat staining his shirt in back. He stood there, wiping his hands. The still, stifling air underlined the anxiousness that everyone felt during his silence.

"His left leg is broken cleanly, right above the knee, and that is good. But his hip on the right side is in bad shape. I can't say whether it is bone or ligament damage. Only time will tell us the full story. But I'm fairly sure that he suffers no internal bleeding, although we must wait and keep a close eye on him for developments. I'm afraid that he'll be in bed for a long, long time."

"But he will be all right, doctor?" asked Alonzo.

"Yes, I believe I can safely say that he will mend in time."

"What happened to him, Doc? Papa is an excellent horseman!"

"He said that Octavio stepped into an armadillo burrow, twisted down to the side, and fell on top of your father, Carlos."

Gulping, Carlos looked at the floor.

Alonzo took charge. "All right, everybody. If we're going to keep this ranch operating, we'll have to get back to work. Pablo, let's get over to the far pasture and try to fill in that burrow. We will see where *Señor* Garcia left off watering the calves. Michael, you, Karl, Rafael, and Juan return to your jobs in the south and east pastures. Carlos, you'd better stay here and help your mother."

"*Sí*. She will need all the help you can give her, *jovencito*," said Pablo.

"Maybe my mom can help out some too," offered Billy, moving toward his horse. "I'll go tell everyone what's up."

Once inside, alone with his mother and his sleeping father, Carlos realized the gravity of the situation. Without Papa to direct things on the ranch, everything could easily get so far behind that they'd never make it to market on time.

Carlos looked into the ashen face of his father and saw the cruel etchings of age — lines that hadn't been there even this morning. "What will happen to us, Mama?"

"Oh, Carlitos. You must grow up so fast now. You are the head of the family until Papa mends. But we must all listen to and help each other. I know that with support from Alonzo and Pablo, we can make it."

"We've got to make it."

That evening, Billy thundered up to the Garcia front porch in a cloud of dust. In his haste, he nearly tipped over the large crocks of freshly made soup that his mother had sent to help the stricken family. No one was in sight, but a dim light shone from the front windows. He guessed that everyone was inside, preparing for dinner. Uncinching the jugs from his saddlebags, he yelled, "Carlos? Carlos! C'mere, quick!"

"SHHHH!! *Por favor*—Papa sleeps! What's the matter?"

"Oh, sorry — I came as quick as I could. Where's Pablo? He's got to clear outta here. Sheriff Taylor is on his way out to see how your dad is!"

Both of the boys knew that the sheriff had been on the trail of Gregorio Cortez after the shooting near San Antonio. He must have been a young man then. But bitter memories lingered and grudges were carried over — sometimes for generations — in these parts, thought Carlos.

"Oh, no! He's inside, helping with the fire. How do we get him out of there without letting him know that we know who he really is?" Carlos had a tremendous sinking feeling in his stomach.

"He'd come if we needed help with something," suggested Billy.

"Quick! What needs doing which wouldn't arouse suspicion?"

"More wood for the fire?"

"He just fetched a load," moaned Carlos. "I've got it! In all of the excitement, we never tended to Octavio. I'm sure he needs a linament rub on his lame leg. C'mon, follow my lead."

The boys entered the house with the soup crocks.

"*Gracias,* Billy. Your mother is so kind," said *Señora* Garcia, taking the jugs from him. "And now I don't need to worry with the evening meal. No need to fight with the cookstove any longer, Pablo. Dinner is here and still hot!"

"Ah, I could eat a bear tonight." He sniffed at the thick, meaty soup and prepared to sit down at the table.

"Pablo, now that I think about how fortunate we really are —" Carlos began.

"*Sí,*" interrupted Billy. "Things could've been much worse . . ."

"I've been wondering how old Octavio held up under

32

the strain," continued Carlos. "He was pretty lame when I brought him home this afternoon."

"Yeah, and you're such a whiz with animals," said Billy, scratching Pepe under his chin, "that maybe a good linament rub would do Octavio a lot of good."

"Well, he's waited this long, he can as well wait until after I've nourished myself."

"But Pablo!" A note of urgency entered Carlos's voice. "He's just a dumb animal, but we've forgotten all about him today. He's a good servant to my father."

Billy took Pablo's hand. They were running out of time. "You know, Pepe would never forgive you if you neglected one of his fellow animals." He was trying to josh Pablo, but he pulled at his arm earnestly.

"All right! All right! It is a sad day when a man cannot sit down to a meal without the badgerings of romantic boys all about!"

"Octavio awaits his hero!" cried Carlos playfully, pushing Pablo from behind while Billy led him out of the room.

"Keep the soup hot, *señora!*" Pablo called over his shoulder, grabbing a lamp with his free hand.

The trio had barely made it into the barn when the sound of approaching hoofbeats reached their ears. Octavio let out a loud, lonely whinny at the sound. The boys increased their persistence.

"Here's a fresh bottle of linament, Pablo . . ."

"I'll get Octavio's stall door . . ."

But Pablo was peering through the dusk, back toward the house, to see who the visitor was. The darkened figure was unrecognizable until the inside lamplight glinted on his silver star. Involuntarily, Pablo ducked back and carefully eyed the sheriff until he was inside.

The boys watched expectantly, then busied themselves inside Octavio's stall when Pablo turned around. He studied them carefully, silently, and then said, "It looks as if the doctor might have told the whole town of

33

your father's accident, Carlitos." He took the bottle of linament from the boy.

"Who was the visitor?" asked Billy innocently.

"Oh, I could hardly see, but I think it might have been a local sheriff." Pablo poured a little linament into his palm and vigorously rubbed Octavio's sore leg. The horse raised his foot in protest, while Carlos calmed him.

"Perhaps he will stay to dinner," suggested Pablo.

He laughed at the crestfallen looks on the hungry boys' faces. "But I expect he merely came to offer your mother condolences on her misfortune. Your father is a sharp businessman with a good reputation around town. I am sure that is why the sheriff came tonight." Pablo continued to rub the linament on the lame leg.

The boys looked at each other. Without words, they knew that Pablo was aware that they shared his secret.

[6]

Several weeks passed with the ranch operations being directed by Alonzo. Work loads doubled as everyone realized exactly how much Carlos's father contributed to the daily activities.

Luckily, the Bakers sent down one of their own hired hands and several more pots of prepared food for the Garcias. Billy had gotten permission to spend much of his time helping out also, much to Carlos's relief.

Carlos had volunteered to take on the bathing of his father, as well as the changing of his splints and dressings. He tried very hard to keep the concern out of his voice when he delivered to his father the news of the day each evening.

"Alonzo took a trip into town today to pick up some hay that came in on the railroad, and Rafael used the roll of wire to fix the south pasture fence."

"Feeding cattle hay in the middle of summer," his father groaned. "This drought is going to break us."

"No, Papa! Everything is going much better than we expected —"

"So, you have found that you can run things around here without me?"

"Oh, Papa . . . you know we need you! Now get some rest before dinner. Mama will be in after a while."

When Carlos got outside, Billy was waiting.

"How is he today?"

"Not much change. He is very bitter and frustrated at being so helpless. It is so hard to talk to him without his taking everything I say the wrong way. What can we do to cheer him up?"

The boys sat on the porch thinking. They were interrupted by the heavy steps of Pablo, scuffing across the dusty yard.

"*Hola, amigos!* Why the long faces?"

"Papa is in the dumps today, Pablo, and we don't know what to do about it."

"Humm . . . Perhaps today will not be a good time for me to talk to him about a request I have."

"If it's something about the ranch, I'm sure Alonzo can answer you," suggested Carlos.

"I have spoken to him already, and he asked that I clear it with your father . . . but it can wait another day."

"Why are you so mysterious, Pablo? What are you going to ask him?" asked Billy, boldly.

Carlos poked him in the ribs with his elbow and gave him a warning glance. It was very bad manners to pry into someone's personal affairs. Carlos felt that if Pablo wanted to tell them, he would, without having to be asked.

But Pablo was laughing, and he eased Billy's dismay. "That's all right, Billy Baker. I don't mind telling you, but you must keep it a secret so no one will ask how old I am. I am having a birthday next week, and would like permission to ride into San Antonio for a few days. I would enjoy a visit with my daughter, who lives there with her family."

"El Rancho del Cibolo will miss you, I bet!" said Billy.

"Oh, with the generous help that your parents sent over, I'm sure that the ranch will survive without me for two or three days." He looked at Carlos, who was deep in thought. "Don't you think so, Carlitos?"

"Well, I don't know. You work three times as hard as anyone else around here. I don't know if Papa will want to spare you."

"Perhaps I shall wait until tomorrow to ask him. When he is in a better mood."

"That's a good idea. He really is in a bad humor today."

When Pablo left, Carlos grabbed Billy by the elbow and dragged him around to the side of the house, away from his father's window.

"I've got a great idea! Something that is sure to cheer Papa up!"

"Well, what is it?"

"A *fiesta!* And Pablo will provide the excuse! Everybody loves a birthday party . . . the only problem we'll have is trying to keep him here instead of letting him go to San Antonio."

"Oh, boy! A real live *fiesta!* I've never been to one before!"

"Well, prepare yourself, *amigo.* A *tejano fiesta* is like nothing you've ever imagined!"

Carlos immediately began planning the surprise. First he talked to Alonzo, who would be helpful in putting off Pablo's request for leave until it was too late. Then he talked to his mother, who began preparing food lists and decorations. Soon, word was out all over the ranch. But everything was kept extremely hush-hush, so that Pablo and Papa would not know what was going on.

As the day approached, excitement mounted and whisperings increased. Alonzo came up with a brilliant idea, which he shared with Carlos and Billy.

"What we need to do is find Pablo's daughter and get her to come here instead of Pablo going there!"

"Great! Do you know anyone who knows her?"

37

"I'm sure I can find a way to get in touch. Consider it done, *jovencito*."

Pablo became more and more anxious as Alonzo piled more and more duties on him. Frustrated and unwilling to give up, even to the last, he continued to badger Carlos about getting in to see *Señor* Garcia and get permission from him.

"He is very bad tonight," Carlos would report. Or he would say, "Papa is sleeping now. The pain has been wearing on him today."

At last, the day arrived, and Alonzo instructed Pablo to accompany him to the farthest calf pasture to set up a branding station. This would be an all-day chore requiring constant attention, so Alonzo knew that Pablo would have no excuse to return to the ranch house.

While the men were gone, decorations were strung in trees and bushes, and food was prepared. Women, finishing the last of their costume embroidery, collected at the party site and helped to fix a mountain of enticing delights. Some of the *vaqueros* dug their instruments from their closets and sat, tuning and strumming. Finally, they practiced a few numbers together.

Fortunately, Papa slept most of the day. But he was not ignorant of the chatter and bustle of activity.

"*Carlos!*" he called, late in the afternoon. "What's going on around here? Is no one attending to the work that needs doing?"

"Papa!" Carlos rushed in breathlessly. "It is a *fiesta!* Pablo is beginning a new year of life today, and we are going to celebrate. Won't it be fun?"

Papa was silent for a moment. "It has been years since we had a party around here," he mumbled. "The last time was when the Castillo boy and his girl got married . . ."

"We thought the time had come again to really put out the effort. We hope that Pablo's daughter is coming in from the city."

"Yes. What a good idea. See if you can get me out

38

onto the porch. Get Rafael or someone to help. Maybe I can do something small to lend a hand."

From the porch, *Señor* Garcia directed the men as they set up tables and chairs in the yard. Gaily colored tablecloths were spread, and the first of the food began to appear from every house in the area. A smoking pit was fired up, and soon the delicious aromas of *cabrito* and beef brisket filled the air.

Carlos and Billy personally picked out the trees between which the *piñata* would be hung. Billy hoisted Carlos up into the tree so he could tie off the fixed end of the rope. After stringing through the wire hanger of the clay pot decorated with paper and filled with candy, the other end of the rope was looped over a high branch, and then tied off at shoulder level, farther down the tree.

"Why don't we just tie this end off like the other?" asked Billy.

"You'll see why later, when the little kids come with their stick to try to break the *piñata*."

At last everything was ready. Lanterns lit the porch, and torches were stuck into the parched earth around the yard. Alonzo and Pablo appeared from the pasture and the music began immediately.

"*Feliz nacimiento,* Pablo!" everyone shouted. The astonishment showed on his face.

"What a surprise! Yes, happy birthday indeed! Happy *fiesta* to you all!"

At the same time, wagons began to arrive along the drive, and crowds of people came in from the city, carrying plates and pots of food. Everyone hugged and congratulated Pablo. His daughter stood proudly at his side, holding his arm affectionately.

Billy's parents could not come because Billy's sister was sick in bed. Fortunately, Billy had gotten permission to stay at the festivities until ten o'clock — long past his usual bedtime. His eyes were wide, filled with rich colors and flashy dancing for most of the night.

Once all of the guests had arrived, the eating began.

Roasted guinea hens, *cabrito, chile con carne,* and beef brisket were served along with potato salad, *frijoles,* rice, and corn pudding. *Tortillas* and *tamales* went with everything, and for dessert, *buñuelos* and *sopapillas* were smothered in honey.

Four men pulled out their instruments and put together an impromptu *mariachi* band. One played a small, four-stringed *vihuela,* one had a bass *guitarrón,* and two had fiddlelike instruments called *guitarra de golpe.* The musicians wore black vests with silver embroidery on them, and red sashes around their waists. The women wore full white, yellow, and red skirts, all with colorful sequins and embroidery along their long hems. Petticoats peeked out below, and polished black shoes completed the costumes.

Finally, someone shouted, "*Vengan niños!* It's *piñata* time!"

"Watch this," said Carlos to Billy.

The children gathered around and argued about who was to be forced to go first (the first one rarely hit the *piñata*). Carlos placed himself discreetly beside the loosely tied end of the string.

One child's clear voice began chanting the familiar *piñata* song, and the others quickly joined in:

> *Yo no quiero oro, ni quiero plata.*
> *Lo que quiero es quebrar la piñata!*

"What are they singing?" whispered Billy.

"They say, 'Gold and silver do not matter — All I want is to break the *piñata!*' "

A mother selected the first participant, blindfolded him, and spun him around. With the other children shouting directions and encouragement, the youngster waved his stick, hitting nothing but thin air. Once, when he got close, Carlos pulled the rope and lifted the *piñata* far out of the child's reach. After a while, a little girl was selected to go next. She waved the stick blindly, with the others laughing and shouting.

Carlos played with them for a while, then an adult took over the rope, lifting the *piñata* high out of reach and lowering it beyond striking distance, depending on how close the children got to the prize. At last, the adults allowed the stick to strike and break the clay pot, and the children were showered with trinkets and candy. A multitude of hands scrambled amid screams and shouts.

Billy was enchanted. Carlos was having fun showing his friend all around the yard, where different activities were occurring at each corner. Over there, a *jarabe* was being performed by a young girl who lifted her frilled petticoats, displaying the flashing steps of her now dusty shoes. In another place, a *vaquero* had pulled out his *concha,* an instrument made of an armadillo shell.

"The song is so beautiful!" exclaimed Billy. "What does it say?"

"He is singing a ballad called a *corrido.* It tells the tale of one of the heroes of the Mexican revolution," answered Carlos.

The evening was capped off by the familiar strains of the Mexican Hat Dance. The boys ran over to where Pablo had tossed down a large *sombrero.* He was prancing around it, clapping his hands. A *señorita* was pushed into the cleared area to dance with him, and they pranced and clapped, slowly at first, but with ever-quickening steps. The music and dancing began to build, with all the crowd clapping the faster and faster rhythm, until finally Pablo grabbed the *señorita,* swung her low toward the ground, and kissed her.

Everyone clapped, laughing, and the boys broke away from the circle, ready to find another enchantment.

"Oops!" said Billy suddenly. "I wonder what time it is? I've got to be back at ten . . ."

"Uh-oh, *amigo.* I'm sure it's past ten by now. Let's ask Papa."

Señor Garcia, propped up in his bed on the porch, looked like a king holding court with his knights. Women flitted around him, serving him food and drinks, and

41

every now and then a musician would come and serenade the crowd from the porch on which he reigned.

"Papa, do you have the time?"

"Why, yes, Carlitos," he beamed. "It's ten-thirty. Why do you ask?"

"Oh, no!" cried Billy. "Pa will have my hide!"

"Don't worry, young one. I will send with you a note explaining what a help you have been to me tonight. Maybe that will ease your problem, *sí*?"

"Thank you, *Señor* Garcia. That would help a lot."

As Carlos walked Billy to his horse, Billy observed, "Your father is in good spirits, *amigo*. Your plan has worked well in every respect."

"*Sí*. I am pleased to see Papa smile for a change. And what a party it has been! Don't worry, I don't believe you'll miss too much. It's about to wind down now, and with so many guests from the city, we'll have to begin looking for places to bed everyone down for the night."

"Hope you don't have to sleep here in the barn."

Carlos shrugged. "If I do . . . *Así es la vida*. I will survive."

"I sure had fun. I'll be down in the morning to help you clean up."

"*Buenas noches, amigo.*"

"*Buenas noches.*"

Carlos watched his friend ride into the night, listening to the quiet, mournful *corridos* being strummed and sung behind him.

[7]

I've been very lucky, thought Carlos as he roused from sleep in his own room, glad to awaken with his hair free of straw. He had narrowly escaped sleeping in the barn with his cousins. Thank goodness most of them are boys, he thought, or else I'd have had to give up my bed to a girl.

He could tell it had been a late night for everyone as he entered the kitchen. Not many people were up, but those who decided to brave the day were slumped at the table, staring blearily into their cups of steaming coffee.

Grabbing a glass of chilled milk, Carlos stepped onto the porch to enjoy his luxury. They rarely had any food as perishable as milk in the house. This jug had been brought to his family as a gift by one of the city-dwelling guests.

The *fiesta* ground was littered with tents and rough lean-tos. One or two people were slowly moving about, but Carlos could hear the harmonies of several different snorers emerging from tentflaps and sleeping pallets.

"Carlitos!"

He jumped at the command. The irritable tone of his father's voice suggested that the *fiesta* may not have soothed the man's spirit after all.

"*Sí*, Papa?"

"It's time to be up. There's work to do! Go get Alonzo and help me onto the porch. Then have him rouse the hands. This is not a summer camp! We've got a ranch to run here!"

Señor Garcia was fidgeting in his bed, trying to slide himself up into a sitting position. Carlos moved to help him with the pillows, but he was waved off. "Go! Do as you're told, son!"

"*Sí, señor.*"

Oh, the bear is loose today, thought Carlos. And we'd best watch our step!

The hands reluctantly assembled while Alonzo and Carlos helped *Señor* Garcia out to the porch. Carlos's mother made the rounds with strong coffee and hard rolls for the men. Guests began to mill in the yard, staying well away from the crowd of working men and their stern taskmaster.

"We've cattle to water and horses to feed, just like always, gentlemen. The yearling calves in the back pasture must be brought in to the feed lot for fattening, and the branding is only half finished. Let's get with it. Alonzo, divide up your teams, but leave Pablo with me. I've a special job for him."

In a scheming voice Carlos whispered to Pablo, "Maybe you'll get clean-up duty with me and the women — drudgery, *sí*, but not as hard as riding horseback . . ."

"Pablo, there's a little sorrel mare out on the ranges that'll be about two this year. I've seen you keeping an eye on her, and she's about due for breaking in to the saddle, so I thought you'd like the chance to do it right."

Carlos watched Pablo's eyes sparkle with anticipation, then dim as he placed his hand to his head.

"Must it be done today, *señor?*"

"No time like the present."

44

Pablo smoothed his erratic curls back from his forehead. *"Sí,"* he whispered.

"And Carlos. You will stay on clean-up detail until all is back to normal."

Carlos thought dismally that it wouldn't be much fun without Pablo to cheer things up. But then again, Pablo wasn't too cheery today anyway. He shrugged. The first thing to do was help the guests pack up their things.

"C'mon, Pepe. Let's get this over with." The hound thumped his tail against the porch floor and rose to follow. Carlos wanted to hurry and finish cleaning up so he could watch Pablo break the mare.

After a time, hoofbeats interrupted Carlos's work. With delight, he looked up to see Billy.

"I've come to help clean up, just like I promised," said his friend.

"Did your father give you any trouble about getting home late?"

"Naw. How's your pa?"

Carlos rolled his eyes. "Back to business as usual. I think perhaps he is not a Garcia anymore — he is *un oso,"* and Carlos pretended to show teeth and claws in a bear stance.

"So give me something to do — as long as it can be done far away from any caged wild animals around here."

The boys worked together until *Señora* Garcia called Billy to help her with some inside chores. Carlos made his bear face again, then he elbowed Billy and said, "Maybe he will be hibernating."

Carlos knocked down and stored tables and lanterns until the sun was high and hot, and drowsiness began to overtake him.

"Hungry, Carlos?" called his mother.

"You bet!"

He ran inside to find Billy relaxing at the table, drinking a cool glass of milk. His feet were propped up on a chair.

45

"Hey, d'you ever do any work?" Carlos asked with resentment.

"Billy Baker has worked hard hauling wood, water, and grain for me, Carlitos," said his mother. "He is being rewarded just as you are." She set a glass of milk in front of her son and went to the stove to fetch some stew.

"Now, both of you eat out on the porch where it is cooler." She laughed at the apprehension that Carlos could not keep from his face. "Your papa is resting in his bed now, Carlitos. It will be safe."

The boys were not on the porch very long before *Señora* Garcia returned, sticking her head through the doorway. "You boys have done such a good job of helping, I think you can take a break and see how Pablo is getting along. I'll tell Papa where you are — but only if he asks!" She laughed and withdrew into the house again. The boys whooped and finished their stew, leaving their empty bowls for Pepe to lick clean.

"I hope Pablo hasn't returned from his errand yet," said Carlos, unable to contain his excitement. "I don't want to miss a thing!"

"What's he doing?"

"You'll see."

When they got down to the paddock, it was empty. By standing on the fence the boys could just see a figure passing through the far pasture, approaching them and leading a second horse.

"There he is," pointed Carlos. "His errand is a special one, *amigo*. He is going to break the sorrel mare!"

"So? What's so special about this mare?"

"Don't you know?" Carlos lowered his voice and looked furtively around them. "It was a sorrel mare that carried the legendary Gregorio Cortez through half of Texas on his flight of 500 miles!"

Billy's eyes widened. "And your dad is letting Pablo break in this mare . . ."

"*Sí* — as a special birthday present for him! I have seen Pablo eyeing this animal when we catch sight of her on the ranges. He holds a special fondness for sorrel mares since the days twelve years ago when he rode so hard and long on a mare so willing!" And then Carlos quoted some of the ballad that the Mexican people wrote to honor Gregorio Cortez.

> All the rangers of the county
> Were flying, they rode so hard;
> What they wanted was to get
> The thousand-dollar reward.
>
> And in the county of Kiansis
> They cornered him after all;
> Though they were more than three hundred
> He leaped out of their corral.

"On the little sorrel mare!" put in Billy.

"Sí. And the saying goes that he reached a high, steep-banked river, like the Cibolo, but it was farther south. And he could only cross it by going upriver seven miles or downriver about ten. But the posse was right behind him, and he had no time. So he whispered in that little mare's ear, encouraging her, and she understood what he wanted.

"They slipped up to the high bank of the river and just leaped off, right into the air, and they fell to the water. When they crossed over, Gregorio had to get them up the far side. So he climbed up the steep bank and carved a narrow path out of the sandy, rocky soil, starting from the top. Then he helped the mare climb up the steep bank."

"Wow! Is that true?"

"That's what they say. The story goes on to tell how Gregorio and the mare rested on the top of the bank, and they heard the bloodhounds come to the other side with the sheriffs and rangers behind them. But none were brave enough to do what Gregorio and the mare had done, so he avoided capture once again.

"When he was rested, and while those who were after him milled around on the other bank, wondering

47

what to do, he fired his pistol in the air and shouted, 'I am Gregorio Cortez! You will never get my weapons till you put me in a cell!' and he rode off into the chaparral."

Billy looked wistfully toward where they could now clearly see Pablo approaching the paddock. "Gee. He really is famous, isn't he?"

"He is a living legend. And you know what, Billy? We know him personally!"

Billy grinned. "Yeah! I never thought of it like that." At Carlos's inquiring glance, he explained, "Well, I'd always just thought of Pablo's real name like a secret — you know, something to be kept quiet. Just between you and me."

"Jovencitos!" called Pablo. Carlos could see, even at a distance, that the weariness had left Pablo. The boys waved energetically.

As Pablo approached, he was talking a blue streak to the mare. She was lathered and a little wild-eyed, but generally calm as she walked along behind Pablo's buckskin gelding. Then he raised his voice to the boys. "She is a spirited one, *amigos!* Plenty of heart — *mucha viveza!* And cunning, too. It took me two hours just to find out where she was hiding!"

He reined up to the gate of the paddock, which Billy and Carlos ran to unlatch for him. As he rode inside, he continued, "Then she led me on a merry chase faster and farther than any of the others in the herd could go! She rides the wind and soars along as if her feet never touch the earth. So I have called her *Águila,* because she moves and thinks like the golden eagle! Don't you, my clever *señorita?* Easy there, now. No one will hurt you, *una pequeña.*"

Carlos smiled at the affection and respect that the man had developed for the mare. It seemed as if she was beginning to trust him.

An extra saddle and bridle sat on the fence, and Pablo led the mare near the tack and tied her loosely to the fence rail. Dismounting and handing his buckskin's reins to Carlos, he said, "And now, we must get you used to all these new things you see around here. Soon you will think of the ranch instead of the range as your home. Carlitos, tie old *Bribón* out of sight, in those trees *por favor*. We don't want any distractions around here, now do we?"

Carlos was amazed that the usually quiet Pablo was finding so much to say to a mere animal. But then again, this mare was no ordinary animal — she was a symbol. When Carlos returned to his perch on the fence rail, he and Billy watched the gentle, patient, painstaking process that Pablo went through to break the near-wild animal to the bit and saddle.

First he held up the foreign objects to her nostrils, which flared in her attempt to identify them. White triangles showed in the corners of her eyes, making her look completely terrified and wild. She snorted loudly as Pablo kept up his running monologue.

He picked up the bridle and showed it to her, allowing her to sniff it some more. Then he untied her and drew the bridle up her foreleg, just letting it touch her red-brown coat. She danced sideways, trying to get her head around to see the horror as it slid up her leg. Always talking, Pablo calmed her, following her prancing stride deeper into the paddock. Then he did the same thing on her other side, and she side-stepped back to the railing.

Though trembling and sweating, the mare finally stopped and allowed Pablo to rub the bridle on her neck, chest, and shoulders. But as he neared her hindquarters, she snorted and once again tried to turn her head around to see what was touching her sensitive flanks. Her skin twitched as if a trillion flies were settling on her and biting viciously.

Carlos saw her ears lay back and was afraid that she was going to strike out at Pablo with a lightning kick. But just as suddenly as the ears went back, they started forward again, then flicked to the side as she tried to figure out what was going on.

At last, when she was no longer twitching and dancing about, Pablo approached her head again and deftly slipped the bridle over her eyes and ears. The bit was in her mouth before she knew what Pablo was doing, and she clomped her mouth open and shut in protest.

"There now, little Águila. That's not so bad, is it? Carlos, could you fetch a bucket of water from the trough? I'm sure our friend is thirsty after all this excitement."

When Carlos returned with the bucket, the horse was still fighting the bit, sticking her tongue out, chomping her jaws, and foaming at the corners of her mouth. The water distracted her for a slight moment, while she bent her head to drink, but the bit was such an intrusion, she could not leave it alone in her mouth.

"I don't think much of the water is getting down her throat," observed Billy.

"She will learn that the bit does not hurt. It is merely a way for her rider to speak to her without words. Oh, yes. She is a smart girl, and she'll catch on fast. Now, let us try leading you about. Come, Águilita, let us get used to all of these nasty things . . ."

Still talking away, Pablo led her around the paddock several times, getting her used to the feel of the leather around her ears, eyes, and muzzle. The boys were hot and dusty, and it wasn't much fun to see Águila walk around shaking her head and lolling her tongue out of the sides of her mouth.

"Let's sit in the shade for a while, Carlos. This is taking much longer than it ever takes Frank to break a horse at my place. He just throws the gear on and broncrides around the paddock until the horse is tired enough to quit."

"Or until he falls off, eh?"

Billy smiled. Neither of the boys liked Frank too much. He was a hard, unforgiving man, and the animals he broke to the saddle most often had broken spirits after Frank was through with them.

They rested, listening to the steady mumble of Pablo, the dust-cushioned padding of the mare as she walked behind him, and the constant buzzing of insects in the shade of the brush they shared. Just as Carlos felt his eyelids grow heavy, Pablo approached the fence where the saddle was soaking up the scorching afternoon heat.

Carlos shook Billy awake and they returned to their vantage point in the sun to see the fireworks. Carlos knew that no matter how gentle a trainer is, a horse will try to reject the saddle by bucking. Things could get exciting.

After offering Águila more water, which she gladly drank with better success this time, Pablo took the blanket from under the saddle and began the rubbing routine again. First the legs, then the shoulders, then the chest and neck, and finally along the barrel toward the flanks. He behaved as if he was wiping her down with any old rag, and when he got to her withers, he settled the blanket on her back and left it there.

Nostrils flaring, she snorted and looked back over her shoulder, sniffing at the inert object on her back. Always talking quietly to the mare, Pablo reached for the saddle and hoisted it near her head. She snorted and backed off, then sniffed some more as he patted her and slapped the saddle. Too heavy to rub along her legs and sides, the saddle would have to be gently slipped directly onto the mare's back.

Pablo eased it along her side, constantly reassuring her with his voice, and slid it into place. She tried to dart from under it, but Pablo was quicker. He stayed right beside her, patting her flanks and the saddle to let her know that it meant her no harm.

Her ears flicked back and forth wildly, and the trembling in her chest and flanks increased. Her sweat quickly lathered under the saddle blanket as she continued to shift and dart, trying to rid herself of this new burden.

51

"If she thinks that's heavy, she ain't seen nothin' yet," whispered Billy.

Pablo quieted her slowly and eased around to her off side to ready the girth. Rubbing and talking, he returned to her left and drew the girth under her chest, cinching it up with authority.

The boys could almost see her fear give way to anger as she decided that she would have no more of this foolishness. In protest, she put her head down and gave the first of many mighty bucks.

Pablo nearly lost control of her front end in his efforts to stay clear of her flailing rear hooves. But he talked and trotted, darting with her when she whipped around and controlling her when she tried to take off running. Each time she threw up her heels, the saddle would give a loud slap as the leathers and stirrups abruptly found their natural resting places. The slaps would further antagonize the mare, and she would buck and twist even more.

"Can we do anything to help, Pablo?" called Carlos when it looked as though the beast would best him.

"No, *amigo* . . . If I lose her . . . get out of the way!"

The boys prepared to flee their vantage point by hanging one leg over toward the safe side of the railing, on the outside of the paddock. She could easily kick them in the heads by mistake if she careened around the enclosure uncontrolled.

But Pablo kept talking and easing her worries and her fury. Slowly, she began to cool off. She finally allowed him to lead her along the railing with more calm than any of them actually felt.

After a complete turn without incident, Pablo rewarded her and himself with a drink of water. "There, now, Águila. Things aren't so bad, are they?"

"How are you ever going to get up on her, Pablo?" asked Carlos.

"She is a spirited one, for sure! But she is also quite smart. I believe she'll know that I mean her no harm. It

53

will just take time. Here's where you can help out a little. But I want you to be very sure you'll be able to get out of the way if she begins acting up. What do you think?"

"Sure, I can help. What do you want me to do?"

"I'm going to begin by just pressing down on the saddle, then I'll lean across it. Then you'll lift me and I'll drape across like a sack of grain. Okay?"

"Sure. Just say when."

"First get on her right. When I say so, push down on the stirrup with your hand. All right? Now."

They each pushed down the stirrup on either side of the saddle, giving the mare the illusion of weight. She skittered and was thrown off balance, but Pablo kept reassuring her.

"Okay. Now, hold the reins while I lean on her. There now, Águilita. I'm not such a big load. I'll stick by you."

Carlos took up the comforting words. "Easy, girl. Take it slow. Everything's all right, now. Easy, now."

Her protests were only half-hearted as she became accustomed to the shifting of the additional weight on her back. Finally, she stopped fidgeting and Pablo relaxed his pressure.

"Billy, come gently and take the reins from Carlos. Now the fun will begin."

With everyone in position, Pablo crooked his leg for Carlos to grab and steady him from the ankle. He leaned his full weight onto the saddle, draped across on his stomach. The mare was thrown off balance again. She shook her head in defiance and turned her head around to look at this latest development. All three of them were murmuring reassurances to her as she sniffed and snorted but stood her ground.

"Now it is time to mount. She will be most surprised when she sees me astride, moving everywhere she does. But until she moves and I follow, and then she masters her fear, she will not understand the entire purpose."

Pablo slipped off again, reassured her while he

brought the reins into position behind her neck, and drew up to the left side again. "Carlos? Give me a leg up."

The boys backed off while Pablo gently adjusted himself in the saddle. He constantly encouraged Águila with his voice and gave her a gentle squeeze to urge her forward.

She took one tentative step, realized that the weight on her back would stick right with her, and threw a fit. With no one to control her head, she took off around the paddock, pitching and bucking, twisting and jerking. She tried every trick she knew to be rid of this latest horror.

Carlos and Billy stood transfixed, watching Pablo keep his seat and maintain his calm stream of encouragement. The mare reached the far side of the paddock, then wheeled and ran like a banshee straight at them.

Carlos was rooted to the ground. As the mare flew like a bullet toward him, he was unable to force his mind to tell his legs what to do. At the last possible moment, he dove at Billy, who was closest to the railing. They both tumbled under the paddock fence.

The mare pulled up suddenly, a split second too late to avoid the fence. Her strong neck pressed against the upper rail as she struggled to regain her balance, rear legs hunched under her far enough that her four hooves nearly touched — only a foot away from where the boys lay in a frozen tangle. The rail gave way with a loud *crack,* and she pitched back in alarm.

Miraculously, Pablo remained astride and the damaged fence rail stayed in the posts, splintered but not broken. The confusion in the mare's eyes was obvious as she stood, vibrating with fear and exhaustion.

Pablo stroked her neck, calming her while the boys got up slowly and backed away. In the same quiet tones, Pablo began addressing them, just as if they were Águila: "You guys came close to scaring us all senseless, didn't you? Why did you not get out of the paddock, as any sensible human would do? I'm certainly glad you are unhurt, but that was a crazy risk to take. There now, girl. This isn't so horrible, is it? Let's just ease around a little longer, and then our first lesson will be over. It won't be as bad next time, *una pequeña* . . ."

Pablo squeezed and the mare moved off uncertainly in the direction he indicated with the reins.

"What happened?" asked Billy in a hoarse whisper. "I stood there and couldn't move! That was the strangest feeling I've ever had."

"Me too! It was like my body was disconnected from my head. I knew in my head that I had to jump out of the way, but my legs never got the message . . ."

"Yeah? Me too. And I thought she was going to come right through the fence on top of us."

Carlos nodded. Still shaking, the boys retired to the shade of the bushes.

After a while, Pablo called to them. "I believe we are ready to return to the barn now, *amigos,* if you will undo the gate. Move gently so she will not get spooked again. Then hop up on Bribón and follow along, well behind Águila. I don't think you'll want to get too near her after your close brush with her hooves," he smiled.

Carlos closed his eyes on the vivid memory of the mare's dusty hooves at his eye level. He smiled uncertainly and moved with Billy to open the gate. Pablo and Águila passed through, and the boys, still drained of all energy, leaned on the fence and watched them pass through the pasture toward the barn.

[8]

Life around the ranch returned to normal after the *fiesta*. Long days of endless work began again, with little time for relaxation or fun. Carlos, with Pepe trotting along behind, was wearily dragging another container of water for the livestock from the still-shrinking river when Pablo rode up on Águila. He had barely been separated from the mare since he roped her in off the range. If Carlos didn't know better, he'd think Pablo slept out in the barn with the mare.

"*Jovencito!* You labor too long. You have some time off for good behavior coming to you. Why not take it now? It certainly looks as though your faithful follower could use a rest too."

They looked back at Pepe, tongue hanging out and his eyes nearly closed from the glare. The dog searched for a little spot of shade under a bush.

Carlos dismounted and leaned against his sweating horse. "The troughs are yet to be filled, Pablo. I cannot leave this chore just now."

"Well then, how about if I help you and make the

57

time go a little quicker? Then we can go off and do something which I promised I'd do for you a long time ago."

"What did you promise? I don't remember."

"Well, lucky for you that I remember, *sí* Carlitos? Come let us finish up quickly."

When the tedious chore was completed, they rested under the semi-shade of a large, gnarled mesquite tree. Their watering tasks had taken them to the extreme border of the property, near the Baker ranch's northwest pasture. Pablo pulled some jerky from his *morral*, shredded it into thirds and handed two to Carlos. "This one's for Pepe," he said. Carlos tore off a piece, offering it to the thirsty dog. For a while, they chewed the peppery strips in silence. The heat pressed upon them like an invisible weight.

Carlos's curiosity surged. "So, Pablo. What is it that you promised and I forgot?"

"A shooting lesson, of course!"

Carlos remembered now. Back in the cemetery, when Pablo had first arrived at El Rancho del Cibolo . . . the copperhead and the gunshot which had saved his life.

"That was a long, long time ago," Carlos stated quietly.

"Only three months, *jovencito*."

"It seems like a lifetime, so much has happened . . ." Carlos was suddenly sad. He felt like something was finished — like an end was near. But he couldn't say exactly what it was that seemed so final.

"Come, *amigo*. Let us use this time wisely. Not much free time is granted during drought season. Look, I brought some targets."

Pablo pulled several old tin plates from his bag. "I found them in your great-great-great . . ." he waved his hand in a rollover pattern to indicate more "greats." Carlos laughed and nodded, saying, "In the adobe, right?"

"*Gracias.* They are probably quite old — but not so old that we cannot blow a few holes in them, *sí?*"

"*Sí.*"

Pablo walked to a point in the fence where he could prop up the plates. Arranging them at different heights along the barbed wire, he was at last satisfied with their positions and returned to where Carlos and Pepe were waiting.

"All of the bullets should go into that rise in the Bakers' field. We do not want to down any cattle with our lesson. Now, hold the pistol like this. Take your other hand to steady it, for it will buck in your hand like a wild *caballo*. Be sure to pull back the hammer, ready to fire. Fix your eyes straight and true on the target and hold your breath deep in your lungs. Then breathe out very slowly and squeeze the trigger as if it is never going to move."

Carlos followed his instructions, and it seemed like an eternity passed before the report reached his ears.

Bang! Carlos's eyes grew wide in shock.

"Wow! That thing really jumps!"

"This time, *jovencito*, keep your eyes open."

Carlos smiled sheepishly. His second shot made one of the plates sing, but he only grazed it.

"Which target are you aiming at, *jovencito?*"

"Second from the right."

"Well, you just hit the one third from the left. Here. Try holding it up a little higher, closer to your line of sight. It will make your muscles feel like jelly, but keep your arms as straight as possible. Eye the nose of the barrel, then focus on the plate. Breathe deeply, hold it, exhale, and squeeze slowly."

Bang! This time he hit the plate at which he was aiming. The impact jarred it loose from the fence.

"Wait, *amigo*. I will fix it."

Carlos rested his arms while Pablo went to wedge the target back in its place.

As the lesson progressed, Pablo had him calling out his intended targets before he shot.

"Third from the right!"

Bang! Zzing!

"Far left!"

59

Bang! Zzing!

"Second left!"

Bang! Plunk!

Finally, he was able to actually hit his aims. But he still had trouble controlling the violent bucking of the pistol when it fired. His arms screamed for rest.

"That's enough for now, *amigo*. Too much shooting will ruin your eyes and your arms."

With a sigh of relief, Carlos handed the pistol back to Pablo. But before they had a chance to sit down, hoofbeats reached their ears. Waiting, they saw two figures appear on their left, out of their previous line of fire but on the Bakers' side of the fence.

Recognizing Billy's mount, Carlos called and waved. "It's Billy and his father," he said to Pablo as they approached the fence. Pepe lifted up his weary head and his tail thumped in the powdery dust. He, too, recognized Billy, and he went toward the fence line to greet him.

"Hola, Carlos!" called Billy, waving and slowing his horse to a jog. When they reached the point where Carlos, Pablo, and Pepe were waiting, Billy said, "Father, this is Pablo, the one I was telling you about. Hey, Pepe, old boy! How're you feeling these days?"

Mr. Baker nodded to Pablo, staring intently into his eyes, studying his face. All at once, tension filled the air.

"Don't I know you, *señor?*" asked Mr. Baker.

"I do not think we have met," answered Pablo, looking down to holster his gun.

Carlos broke in, trying to change the subject. "Pablo was teaching me how to shoot his pistol. I was getting pretty good at it too!"

Billy brightened. "Wow! I've never shot a handgun before."

The boys watched the men stare at each other then look away in forced politeness. Finally, Mr. Baker said, "We were riding the fences and heard the shots."

"We figured it was some target practice," said Billy. "But I never thought you'd beat me to the punch in learning how to shoot, *hermano.*" The boys saw the men again stealing glances at each other.

"Isn't it a great idea?" bubbled Carlos, still trying to distract the adults. Pablo remained silent, sometimes looking at the plates with their ragged holes, and sometimes staring a long time at the horizon, but still shifting his eyes occasionally to Mr. Baker's face. Billy's father fixed his stare along the fence and into the pasture, over his shoulder and up at the sky, always taking sidewise glances at Pablo.

"How is your father today, Carlos?" asked Billy.

"Oh, he seems in brighter spirits, but he's still discouraged at having to be motionless when so much needs doing."

"Does Alonzo need any extra hands to help out?" asked Mr. Baker, his attention returning to the conversation.

"So far, we're able to manage. With Pablo's help, and some traveling *vaqueros,* we're doing all right, considering the circumstances. Thank you for asking, *señor.*"

"Well, you tell him that if there's anything he needs, just send word through Billy, and we'll do whatever we can."

"Gracias, señor."

"Well, guess we'd better get along," said Mr. Baker after a long pause. "It was good meeting you . . . Pablo."

Helplessly, Carlos watched Billy look over his shoulder at him and shrug as they rode away. The tension lifted, but in its place was left a vital need to hurry.

"What was that all about?"

"Amigo," began Pablo. "We must talk. Time is running short." He appeared very nervous.

"Time for what is running short?"

"Let us sit down again under this tree."

Pablo was silent awhile, fingering his *morral.* "I'm afraid that Billy's father recognized me. As I recall, your father said that *Señor* Baker had pursued me as a member of the posse."

61

With this frank admission, Carlos knew that it was pointless to play innocent. Obviously, Pablo knew that Carlos was aware of his true identity.

"Even if he doesn't remember whose name matches this face now, he will in a few days," continued Pablo.

"But you've changed . . . You must look different than you did then. He'll never put it together! And he's changed too. Maybe it doesn't matter to him now." Nibbles of doubt entered Carlos's mind even as he said the words. Then he remembered Billy repeating what his father had called Gregorio — "Sheriff Slayer," he had said.

"And anyway, that was twelve years ago," Carlos continued. "What can anyone do about it now — today?"

"Nothing, against me. But he is a powerful man. He could make things very difficult for your father."

"No! The Bakers are our friends. They would have no reason to harm us!"

"I have heard that Billy's father was also a friend of the dead sheriff — the second one that I was accused of shooting. Old grudges die slowly in this hard land, *amigo*."

They were silent a moment.

"So what are you going to do?" Carlos looked down at the ground he was sitting on. A lone, persistent beetle was braving the sun and heat, foraging among the jagged pebbles and scrubby grasses near their shade. Carlos watched the tireless, jerking motions of the insect as it encountered a pebble, then backed off, trying another route, where it would run right into another, larger pebble. Again it would change direction and go around, only to hit another obstacle.

Tiring of the beetle's dogged activity, Carlos avoided looking at Pablo's face. Thoughtfully, his gaze was drawn to a column of smoke rising in the distance, off to his right. He mulled over the meaning of what Pablo had said — and worse, what he might say.

"I'm afraid that the time has come, *jovencito*. I must make a very difficult decision —"

Pepe began barking and whining. He left his resting place under the tree and trotted in the direction of the ranch house. Strange that he'd leave without us, thought Carlos, who was no longer listening to Pablo. His mind finally recognized what his eyes had seen a moment ago — what Pepe already must have known. Smoke always means fire.

"Pablo, look!" Carlos pointed over his friend's shoulder.

In a flash, they were both mounted and galloping toward the billowing, dark, evil smoke which was no longer just a column. It was becoming a wall, spreading faster than their horses could run.

[9]

They reached a scene of chaotic activity. People were running and racing in every direction. Shovels were flying, digging an enormous trench around the house. Many of the women and children were piling into a readied wagon, and soon they raced, in a billow of dust, away from the spreading brushfire. Horses and cattle, freed from stalls and paddocks, were running around wild-eyed, whinnying and mooing. Directions were being flung by Alonzo and *Señor* Garcia, and everyone was scurrying in a frenzy.

There was little water around to fight the frightful flames. Fortunately, Carlos had filled all the troughs, so details of men were sent to the accessible fields to try to recover the water. When they returned, buckets appeared from everywhere. Rows of men lined up, passing the half-filled containers from hand to hand, desperately trying to keep the flames from the yard of the ranch house. One bucket brigade was intent upon soaking and resoaking the roof of the house to ward off any stray sparks.

"Curse the wind!" cried Pablo, as he watched the flames blow closer and closer to the house. "Hurry, Carlos! Untack your horse and let him run so he can fend for himself." Águila was already half-tackless and ready to bolt toward safety, wherever that might be.

Carlos and Pablo quickly entered the fray. The roar of the flames was almost unbearable to Carlos, and his arms ached from the strain of passing buckets. Pepe ran about, trying unsuccessfully to herd the loose livestock. As the protective trench grew, the piles of dirt were placed on the fire's side of the barrier. Alonzo was red in the face, trying to shout loud enough to be heard.

"Keep some of that dirt on this side of the ditch! If the fire leaps the barrier, we'll need it to douse whatever we can. The water won't last forever! Chop down that mesquite tree over there . . ."

Carlos saw that Rafael couldn't hear him, so he broke out of the bucket line and raced to the barn for the axe. He pitched the tool to Rafael just as Alonzo shouted, "and get all the brush across the trench to the fire's side."

Out of the corner of his eye, Carlos saw Billy and Mr. Baker race up. They spoke briefly with *Señor* Garcia, confined to his chair on the porch, then gathered a few men into a crowd. Carlos ran and joined the group, getting quick instructions from Mr. Baker.

"*Señor* Garcia says that the largest part of the herd is in the southeast pasture. We're going to try to herd them toward the flames near enough to get through the gate to the north, then turn them back to the south again and cut the fence through to my property. Perhaps they can find safety then, as the wind is pushing the flames to the north. Let's go."

Catching and retacking the mounts was more of a challenge than anyone had expected. As the crackle and roar of the flames licked closer and closer, the noise and smoke confused the horses. Carlos found himself again racing into the barn, this time to fetch some grain with which to tempt them. At last, Carlos had Bribón and

Águila under control, and he grabbed Pablo to go with them.

"Come. Valuable time has been wasted," said Carlos. "Your experience as a *vaquero* is needed. We must follow Alonzo and Mr. Baker."

Pablo started at the mention of Billy's father, then threw a saddle on the mare's back, cinched it up, and mounted. Several of the selected men were still coaxing the shying horses to them, so Alonzo shouted, "Come and help when you can. We're going on!"

Off they galloped toward the southeast, into the wind. No one asked how the fire started, but Carlos wondered. There had been no lightning, so he assumed that someone had been careless. Boy, he thought. I wouldn't want to be that person when all this is over.

When they reached the pasture, the cattle were near panic. All huddled together in a lowing, swirling mass, they turned one way and saw the flames. In another direction, they could smell the smoke. Off to the east, they could see a sturdy fence.

"They're real nervous, boys. Let's all be careful," said Mr. Baker.

"We must ease them toward the gate, which is also toward the flames," instructed Alonzo. "We'll have to try to move them slowly, so they'll stay together and not race away."

Everyone quickly got into position. Carlos's heart was beating in his throat. The tension was enormous.

"Hey, Billy!" Carlos called. "You scared?"

"Naw!"

"I sure am!"

"Yeah. Me too." Billy grinned.

Suddenly, a piercing whistle sounded from Alonzo, and the cattle drive was on. Carlos slapped his thigh with his reins and gave a sharp whistle. "C'mon, there. Hi-yup! Hi-yup!" He eased his horse toward the mass of cattle, trying to turn their heads toward the north. He rode up ahead for a bit, encouraging them to follow. Then he circled back and eased forward again.

Despite the efforts of the *vaqueros,* the cattle were reluctant to face the flames. As the ones in front turned toward the back in fear, the ones in back were urged forward by the men. The group became tighter and tighter. More lowing emitted from the center, and a few confused steers near the edges broke away from the mass, running toward daylight.

Twice the herd was edged forward, and twice it fell back in segments that the *vaqueros* strained to group back together. Sweat poured off of Carlos's face. The heat and concentration were sapping his strength. He could sense that the breaking point of the cattle was very near his own. The tension crackled in the air like the flames which were driving the cattle mad.

"We must cut the fence wire!" yelled Pablo. "Let them go out toward the west, then perhaps we can turn them toward the south and into the Bakers' fields."

"Hurry, bring the cutters!" shouted Alonzo.

Several men rode over to the fence and dismounted. While one snipped the wire, two caught the ends and tried to carefully roll them back toward the closest posts. There were at least eight strands of barbed wire to cut, so Carlos and Billy helped the others maintain the herd through the tedious procedure.

Suddenly, an observant cow saw the opening grow in the fence. As if on her cue, the entire left side of the huge herd surged toward the fresh opening, engulfing Billy's mount. The men who were on the ground cutting the fence ran for their lives as their horses shied away, outracing the frenzied cattle by a hair. Billy's horse, caught up in the middle of the mass of cattle, reacted to the race and stampede by rearing dangerously.

"Hold on, Billy!" screamed Carlos, who was on the safe side of the sea of beef. He watched Billy grope for his horse's mane, drop his reins, and lose control. But the horse came back down to the ground with Billy still astride. Then it took off like demons were following it.

"Lie low, Billy Baker!" shouted Pablo, riding with the stampede. He slowly closed in on Billy and his confused horse. "Stay close to his neck in case he rears again!"

After what seemed like an eternity, Carlos saw Pablo catch up to Billy's galloping horse and grab the boy off his saddle. With apparent ease, Pablo and Billy worked their way out of the herd just before the last of the animals funneled out of the makeshift opening.

"Boy, that was close!" said Carlos breathlessly when he caught up to them.

"Carlos, quick! Take Billy back to his house. I must race to help turn the herd toward the south! If only we had more *vaqueros!*" And suddenly, Pablo was gone.

"How do you feel, *hermano?*"

"A little shaky," Billy gulped.

"Can you keep on going?"

"They sure need our help — only, it would've been better if I'd been able to keep a hold on my horse."

"Hang on!"

The boys galloped after the dust and rumble of the stampede. Carlos could hardly see where they were headed through the cloud they kicked up. To make matters worse, the cruel wind shifted and came straight out of the east, engulfing the herd in billows of smoke.

"Oh, no! The wind!" cried Carlos.

"I bet the fellows at the house are relieved by the shift," suggested Billy, close to Carlos's ear. Grunting, Carlos pressed Bribón harder.

In despair, the *vaqueros,* still following the herd, watched the cattle turn north rather than south in the confusion of the dense smoke. The fire kept marching across the parched pastures, now heading toward the river, which was to the left of the stampede. With a vicious gust of wind, the fire raced west ahead of the leading *vaqueros* and finally cut them off from any direct approach toward the cattle.

"Quick! To the Cibolo!"

They all turned hard to the west, trying to beat the fire before it reached the banks of the river. Carlos knew that there was yet a hope that the fire might allow the herd to run directly north, along the deep gully cut by the Cibolo.

"Por favor, a Dios," he whispered, over and over, in rhythm to the beat of his exhausted horse's hooves.

"Look, Carlos. They're stopping — " began Billy. They watched as the men who were already at the high banks of the river stopped and hung their heads. Carlos's heart dropped into the pit of his stomach.

"Oh, no . . ."

Pablo turned toward them as they rode up, anguish written across his face. Suddenly, his frustration and fury exploded over them.

"I told you boys to go home! What are you doing here? Come! We must go. Now!"

Pablo herded them around as if they were a stray steer. But Pablo was not so quick that Carlos and Billy did not see the panicked cattle, one after another, plummeting over the bank of the river to their deaths on the rocks below.

[10]

Early the next morning the fire burned itself out. Devouring everything in its path until it hit the slash of the Cibolo, it finally ran out of combustible material on which to feed. With the wind steadily from the east during the night, and with every able-bodied man in the county there to contain it on the north and south, the fire had died like the cattle it had killed, at the banks of the Cibolo.

Bone-creaking tired, Carlos dragged himself to the singed ranch house. The surrounding trees looked spotty, with patches of naked limbs, blackened leaves, and unharmed green areas. They had been mighty lucky to have been able to save the house and barn. Everything surrounding them was black and wispy with ash and smoke. Carlos looked through bleary eyes at the devastation around him. He stumbled into the house and, with relief, closed out the terrible sight and dropped immediately to sleep.

The sound of gunfire in the distance roused him. His body screamed in protest as he tried to sit up in bed. His head thumped and his eyelids felt lined with sand. Groaning, he flopped back down again.

His stomach voiced its disapproval by growling loudly. Carlos propped himself up again. Judging by the sun, it was already past midday. "I haven't eaten since yesterday morning," he moaned, half-aloud, rubbing his empty stomach. The smell of stale smoke, sweat, and ashes assaulted his nostrils. "Oh, these clothes! *Oloroso por las nubes* . . . phew!" As he ripped off the offensive garb to change into something a little fresher, Carlos realized that he was no longer hungry. And then he heard another rifle shot.

"Papa?" he called. There was no one about. Wondering how his father could be anywhere but in his bed or on the porch, Carlos went to the barn to see if any of the loose horses had been rounded up. There was only one which had not been used yesterday during the failed round-up. Carlos tacked the mare up and called to Pepe. The old hound edged around from the shady side of the house's foundation and swung his tail in recognition.

"Come, old boy. Let's see what all the commotion is about."

Following the sound of sporadic shots, they crossed the blackened fields toward the river. The sun beat down without mercy on the ravaged earth. Nearing the banks of the Cibolo, Carlos felt an uneasy twinge in his chest. He pulled up his mount, jumping at the report of another rifle shot.

"I don't think I want to see what they're doing, Pepe." He could not voice his suspicion that some of the cattle had survived the plunge to the rocks. Nausea rolled in his stomach, and Carlos turned his mare away from the river. A tear escaped his eye and rolled down the side of his nose. He looked at Pepe, remembering when a similar fate had threatened the ailing dog.

From the little rise on which he stood, he looked back over the devastation. The enormous loss that his family had suffered in less than twelve hours began to settle into his mind. He felt betrayed, alone, lost, and tired — so very tired.

Another rifle shot behind him made Carlos jump again. He shook himself out of his self-pity. "I'd better go find something I can do to help clean up," he told Pepe.

He was working on corralling some of the strays when Billy rode up, breathless and red-faced.

"Is your family all right?" asked Carlos, alarmed.

"He knows!" breathed Billy. "Today at lunch, I heard Pa mention Gregorio's name. I think he knows that Pablo is Gregorio."

"Did he look angry?"

"I didn't stop to find out. I just heard the name and came to warn you. They don't even know I'm gone yet."

"Is he coming here?"

"I don't think so — at least, not until your father returns from town."

"So that's where everybody is! Did Pablo go with him?"

"I don't know. Pa said something about your father and Mr. Carter, the banker. I guess they're down there talking business."

"C'mon, let's find Pablo."

The boys rode over to the little adobe where Pablo was staying. Águila was nowhere to be seen.

"Maybe he's with the others at the riverbank," suggested Carlos.

"What are they doing . . ."

Carlos looked at Billy, and his friend looked away as he realized.

"Pablo?" Carlos called.

They dismounted and knocked on the door. "Pablo?"

No one was inside, so Carlos went to the window to peer in.

"C'mon, Carlos. He's not here. Let's go look down in the paddock. Maybe he's working with Águila or something."

"I don't think we'll find him, *amigo*. Look."

Billy cupped his hands around his eyes and looked

through the dusty window. There was a white sheet of paper on the small table inside.

The boys entered the adobe and sat down on the makeshift cot with the letter.

> Old man trouble has followed me through my life, and he found me here, at El Rancho del Cíbolo. I know that I can do you and your father more good by leaving than by staying.
>
> I'm sorry to have to go this way, but I hate to say *"adiós."* I can do no more good here. My friend, your father, has suffered enough, so I've taken this time to move on in his absence.
>
> Go to the hollow tree where we first met. You will find a parcel there by which you can remember me. What was once given to me by friends, I now give to you in friendship. Take care, *jovencito*. Take care.
>
> Your friend, Gregorio Cortez
> P.S. Águilita is with me.
> I pray you will understand.

A single tear rolled from Carlos's eye onto the letter. Billy threw himself back on the cot and said, "I can't believe he's really gone."

"Believe it, *amigo*. He's gone."

The boys mounted their horses in front of the empty adobe. There was some commotion at the main house, so they rode that way slowly.

"Carlitos!" called his father. "Where is Pablo? There's someone here I'd like him to meet."

Carlos regarded the stranger closely and saw on his jacket the five-pointed star within a solid ring, hand-cut from a Mexican ten-peso silver piece. The word "Texas" was etched across the star, while "Rangers" circled the lower rim.

"I don't know, Papa. I haven't seen him all day," replied Carlos calmly.

"I knew your friend Pablo many years ago, son," said the man. "He was a friend of mine down south. We almost grew up together. I knew him by another name, though." Carlos's heart stopped with the fear that this stranger would utter the name he had kept such a closely guarded secret for all these months.

But the man hesitated and said, "Yep, he always was a loner. Maybe he's moved on again." After another pause he added, "Still, he usually manages to leave a little piece of himself behind. He is a good man."

Carlos shrugged, pretending that it didn't matter to him. "You are a Ranger, *señor?*"

"Yes. I was called in last night from over in Karnes County to help out any way I could with the fire. Unfortunately, I got here too late. Your father spoke highly of all the *vaqueros* and neighbors who pitched in to help. But he mentioned especially a man on a sorrel mare."

"*Sí.* He is a fine help around here with so much to do. But I have not seen him yet today. There is a clean-up crew at the riverside, but I have not been there."

The man placed a large, calloused hand on Carlos's knee. "I will go there and check for him."

As the man rode off, Carlos and Billy eased their mounts from *Señor* Garcia's view, then took off like lightning toward the hollow pecan tree.

"Maybe we can catch Pablo before he can go too far," called Carlos, over his shoulder to Billy. "We've got to tell him that he can stay without fear!"

But when they arrived at the tree, all was quiet. The once-rushing river below was silent, and they knew there'd be no fishing for a long while. There was no sign of Pablo, nor any trail or hoofprints to indicate the direction he had taken.

"Well, let's look in the tree, at least," said Billy in an impatient tone.

"But we've missed him!"

"Maybe whatever's in the tree will tell us where he went!"

Carlos had to stretch up from his stirrups to reach the high hole. His hand fell on a small leather sack, which he withdrew and opened. Inside was a yellowed paper, folded and refolded many times along the same lines.

"It's some sort of map," whispered Carlos.

"Let's see."

The boys studied the faded lines for a moment, then Billy said, "Yeah, here we are. This big tree down here is what our hollow tree used to look like. And over here is the river."

He stopped pointing when Carlos grabbed his arm. With eyes bugging out of his head, Carlos whispered, "Gregorio's treasure!"

Billy's eyes widened. "Do you think so?"

"What else could it be?" He bent again to the map. "Then this four-zero is . . ."

"It must be the paces from the tree to a big stone over there."

When they looked toward the place indicated by the map, all they could see was a thick tangle of mesquite and prickly pear.

"What do you want to bet there's a stone under all that growth," said Carlos, getting excited. They dismounted near the clump and Billy felt around blindly with his boot. His heel scraped something hard.

"Yep! There's a big rock under here all right. Now where?"

"Ten paces northeast, toward . . ." he looked up and scanned the horizon for something that resembled the rough picture on the map.

"Toward your great-great-great-great-grandfather's adobe!" exclaimed Billy, straining to look over Carlos's shoulder. "See, that little square with the squiggles is a chimney with smoke coming out! I bet that house was occupied twelve years ago, and they never even knew Gregorio Cortez was out here, burying his treasure!"

They paced off the interval, keeping the distant roofline of the adobe in sight. Then they headed fifty paces toward an ancient, gnarled mesquite tree, and turned a little more west, toward a large outcropping of rock near

75

the banks of the river. Finally, a little "X" was placed on the map, another twenty-five paces away, near what looked like a yucca plant on the paper. The boys looked around and saw nothing that resembled the drawing.

"I wonder how accurate the directions on this map are," mused Billy.

"Well, he was on the run, remember. I'm sure that this is very rough. And after twelve years, the yucca could well be long dead and disintegrated. I guess we'll just have to head sort of north and a little east again."

"But remember, his paces are a little longer than ours, so add one or two to the end."

"Okay. Ready? One, two, three, four . . ."

When they reached the suspected spot, they each dropped to their knees and started digging frantically. After a while, Carlos stopped and studied the map again.

"Boy, I wish we'd brought a shovel," said Billy, inspecting his sandy hands. The ground was so hard and parched they could make little headway.

"Well, he didn't have a shovel back then. It can't be too deep."

"Yeah, but there hadn't been a five-month stretch without water back then either."

"Let's try to find a stick."

They scanned the banks of the river until they found a pair of likely digging instruments. With renewed vigor, they dug in their designated spot, but found nothing.

"Maybe we're too far east," suggested Billy.

"Or west or north or south," grumbled Carlos. "Without that final marker, the hole could be anywhere around here."

They stopped for a minute and rested.

"If the yucca was big enough to use as a marker twelve years ago, it must have had a large trunk," suggested Billy.

"Yeah. Maybe if we can find the trunk stump, or a definite root system, we'll locate the area a little easier."

With their sticks they began scoring lines in the

earth where they thought the yucca must have been. When a good-sized grid had been marked out, Billy's stick hit an obstruction.

"Hey, over here. Let's dig a little and see if it's a stump or a rock."

Sure enough, they uncovered a hard, dried circle of wood, with a large root going off deep to the right. The inside of the plant had rotted away.

"So, it must be here — we were only off by about a foot!" said Carlos.

Tired and dusty, they tried digging one more time. Carlos had chipped out only about two or three inches of earth when his stick hit a hard surface.

"I think it's a rock," he said wearily. The sun was roasting them from above while the ground reflected the heat back up from below. He sat back on his heels and rested a moment. Then Carlos dug around on one side of the obstruction and found it to be unnaturally smooth.

"Hey, I think it's a crock or a bowl . . ."

Billy began helping him with his discovery. At last, they could lift the container from the earth. Underneath the domelike protection of the bowl, they saw the remains of a leather *morral*.

Carefully, Carlos cradled the ancient package up to ground level and opened the top. One of the draw-leathers broke, and a hole opened along the seam of the rotting leather. But inside, in perfect condition, were coins and jewelry — anything that the Mexican people could think to give their hero when he suddenly appeared in the night twelve years ago, asking for their help.

"He left you his treasure," breathed Billy. "Now the ranch can be saved."

Carlos shook his head in disbelief. "I thought it was just a story . . ."

He fell silent for a moment, then looked at Billy and spoke softly, "Only the river knew the real secret of Gregorio Cortez."

Glossary

abrazo — a hug
adobe — sun-dried brick made of clay; a house made of these bricks
adiós — goodbye
águila — eagle
alaba el cielo — praise heaven
amigo — friend
así es la vida — such is life
ayuda — help
bribón — rascal
buenos días — good day
buenas noches — goodnight
buñuelos — corn fritters, usually dipped in honey or syrup
caballo — horse
cabrito — the meat of a young goat
chile con carne — chili with meat
concha — a mandolin-like instrument with four pairs of strings; made from an armadillo shell
corrido — a ballad; a tale told in musical form
curandera — a medicine woman; healer
El Rancho del Cibolo — The Ranch of the Cibolo (River)
feliz nacimiento — happy birthday
fiesta — party
frijoles — beans
gracias — thank you
guitarra de golpe — fiddle; violin
guitarrón — guitar
hermano — brother
hermanos de la sangre — brothers of the blood (blood brothers)
hidalgo — Spanish nobleman
hola — hello

jarabe — a high-stepping, foot-stomping dance
jovencito — young man
mariachi — musical group
médico — doctor
morral — nosebag; usually used as a kind of knapsack
mucha viveza — lots of life; very lively
niños — children
oloroso por las nubes — smelly to the clouds (smells to high heaven)
oso — bear
para siempre — forever
perrito — little dog
piñata — clay pot covered with colorful paper and filled with candy and trinkets (now usually made with paper-maché)
por favor — please
por favor a Dios — please, God
pronto — quick; quickly
señor — Mr., or sir
señora — Mrs., or madam
señorita — Miss, or young lady
serape — a blanket that covers the shoulders
sí — yes
siesta — afternoon rest
sombrero — hat
sopapillas — flour puffs, usually filled with butter and honey
tamales — a meat or sausage mixture rolled in cornmeal, then wrapped in corn husks and baked or steamed
tejano — a person from Texas, usually referring to the earliest residents of Mexican origin
tortillas — flat, thin cornmeal or flour cakes
una pequeña — little one
vayáte — get out of here
vaqueros — Mexican cowboys
vengan — come
vihuela — a four-stringed strumming instrument
yegua — mare